JĀNA

a novel

by

Mi'Kha-el Feeza

1st Edition

Book **2** *of 3*

Sun Shone

Search for Truth

a "RA Specialty, Inc." project

羽 很 不朽 **Publishing Company**

Book Age Appropriate Rating:
PG-23 (Parental Guidance till Age 23)

Copyright © Mi'Kha-el Feeza. All Rights Reserved.

Please respect the Integrity of the artist so that the artist can continue to thrive to bring you more works of art!

Piracy affects both the livelihood of the author, publisher, and all those that have collaborated to bring you this piece of art. Thank you!

EF Publishing Book 2 of 3 of Jana Trilogy Novel International Identification Alpha/Number:

7March1968JanaTriologyBook2of3RT13APRIL1950-PB

Everlasting Feather Publishing Company (EF Publishing) WEBSITE:

EverlastingFeather.Com

Thank you for your support! Jana Trilogy **eBook available**. Check with your favorite Book App or contact us.

Mi'Kha-el Feeza WEBSITE:

Eternoi.Com

Buenos días Reader!

Regeneration of Love and Resistance for the common good is working at my website. We are looking for like-minded individuals and organizations to collectively help tackle the ills of our communities in this world to bring true change peacefully to all its inhabitants! If you'd like to join one of our committees, please do so! We are a true Volunteer Based organization. Every Member is a Volunteer, including leadership! Sincerely, Mi'Kha-el Feeza

eternoi@protonmail.com

This 2nd book of the novel Jana is dedicated to Malcom X. A man for the people and for peace. Malcom X was a visionary that we should all aspire to achieve to help make this world a better place for all humanity, not just the select few.

A brotherhood and sisterhood mentality encompasses this great man called Malcom X.

Thank you Malcom for never giving up! A role model for every human being. Amazing you are Malcom X! Amen.

Sincerely, Mi'Kha-el Feeza

J ā n a
Trilogy Book 2 of 3 **Table of Contents**

▦ ▦ ▦ ▦ ▦ ▦ ▦ ▦
▦ ▦ ▦ ▦ ▦ ▦ ▦ ▦

PART **3** of 7
A MIXTURE OF PLEASURE AND PAIN

*Note: **Part 3 of 7** has **Chapter Fourteen,** A Proposition, **Chapter Fifteen** Intensification Of The Dream, **Chapter Sixteen** The Unexpected News, and **Chapter Seventeen** A New Resolution, in Book 1 of 3 of Jana Trilogy novel.*

The last chapter (Chapter 18) in this Part 3 of 7 is found here in book 2 of 3 of the Jana trilogy novel:

PART **4** of 7
PRESET COMPONENTS OF
THE UNFOLDING JOURNEY

PART 5 of 7
JANA'S TRANSFORMATION

And now begins **Book 2** of 3 of
J ā n a
trilogy novel…

Chapter 18
Jana Begins Her Novel
(The Story Develops)

The next morning, Jana sat alone on the bed with the laptop on her lap.

llap lap laptop lap

Jana was thinking how to start her adventure into the *literary* realm.

Jana began to get frustrated at not coming *up* with any ideas to begin her story about a Native American boy.

Jana decided to *close* her *eyes* and repeat:

 "*One is one*"

"*One is one*"

"*One is one*"

.....Then she held her presence *still* in silence.

Then, Jana began to write:

The sun shone on the plains as a boy of five stood looking forward toward his parents as they worked the ground. The boy was from a native Comanche tribe who had, by 1801, begun to plant more corn this year than the previous...pursuing a more sedentary existence. They were able to sell their goods better now that the white man had introduced the horse over 250 years prior.

The family of the boy were happy although at times they had to fight off neighboring tribes and the increasingly encroaching white man who came closer and closer to their land.

The boy named Standing Bow was named after his curve like posture and early wantings to stand-up right after birth.

Through observation the boy knew, now at five, that the white man was not willing to respect his kind. Standing Bow had heard his father speak of other tribes further north east who were fighting off the white man. He also heard of how the white man deliberately killed off the buffalo and let them rot---not using neither hide nor meat nor bone.

Standing Bow was young but very observant since early on—he was able to speak by two years old---something that not even girls at that age could do...at that age the girls could construct verbal words to communicate at a very rudimentary level. But Standing Bow could talk more advanced...speaking in a very complex contemplative manner.

Standing Bow was no usual child who often did not get along with the other boys in his tribe. He was a loner who was always in contemplation. When he spoke he usually only spoke about everyday normal matters.

It seemed though that his complex thoughts superseded what he actually said verbally. The rare complex verbal encounters his father experienced with Standing Bow one day revealed complex thought when his son began speaking about matters concerning planting seeds. His father thought his son processed more than what he usually spoke. It was as though his son wanted to keep his extraordinary abilities concealed.

His father said nothing about it---he knew that his son was gifted in thought but did not want to require him just yet to discuss all that ran in his mind.

His father loved him and wanted the best for him. Mother was also aware of her peculiar son who did not play with the other boys in the tribe. She too decided it was best to wait and to see when the boy was ready to share his thoughts.

The family had gone through many hardships in the past, having to deal with tornadoes that nearly took their lives during the spring time. They knew of the dangers of the winds and built tunnels eight feet under to hide in when it was imminent that a tornado was on its way. This protection however did not protect their crops that were usually destroyed by roaring tornadoes that knew no boundaries.

Standing Bow was the only child the family had. Previously, the couple had one son who was taken from them by a warring faction that felt no remorse in removing the child from the tribe. He was one of five that had been kidnapped.

The tribe had ran after the thieves, but not having horses at the time, they could not catch up to these perpetrators who did have horses. But the tribal leaders did not give up. The tribe took on foot for three days in the direction of the horse tracks the thieves left behind.

On the third day they reached the

> raiders and ambushed them, killing all six men with their knives and arrows. The thieves had guns, but they proved ineffective in a moonless midnight ambush. To their dismay, the tribe did not find the children. They were told by a woman that accompanied the thieves that the children had been sold to a group of white men who traded them for 10 rifles and some ammunition.

Jana sat there thinking of the sadness of *losing* a child. She had begun to feel more and more attached to the *being* within her. To lose a child, she now felt, was to lose your life.

Jana was surprised on how the words flowed from her mind to her fingers to the electronic paper in front of her.

As Jana sat there, ideas started to flow more and more and she decided to write these down on paper in an outline format to help her remember them for later.

Jana decided to stop writing at least for now.

Moving toward the edge of the bed Jana placed her feet on the ground and placed the laptop on top of the small *light*-table near the bed.

She stood up and stared at the wall.

Jana was in deep thought and was excited about finally being able to start her story: into a *journey* she would blaze...creating a track into her mind leading into her inner workings; a track that would (she hoped) lead her to a better understanding of herself as a human being... here on this planet (this *prism)*.

Jana felt comfortable with her new freedom to contemplate: having the TIME NOW to think.

TO THINK*!*

Many times in the past she had woken up as a teacher...living her life as a teacher. Jana was completely immersed in this profession.

For nearly *9* years her mind during a school year was on *being a teacher*; and after work reflecting on *being a teacher* and preparing for the next day on *being a teacher*.

The TIME NOW was truly a breath of fresh air.

There stood Jana: breathing in the information flowing from her mind...coming to realizations on avenues of Wisdom that would lead her to The Truth.

PART 4 of 7
PRESET COMPONENTS OF
THE UNFOLDING JOURNEY

Chapter Nineteen
Wild Feather
Pinhole-View of the
Upbringing of Jana's Father

Wild Feather stood there in the plains of the Oklahoma Reservation at the age of five.

F I V E

He stood outside in the cold-winter-December feeling alone and lost.

The young boy Wild Feather could not see beyond his **presence** since for a child there is no beyond but what you have in front of you.

Wild Feather felt the coldness creep into his fingers and bare toes. He wore some rags of mud white with tears-at-the-seams. [double meaning]. He had not gone to school yet and did not know it was coming.

His initial behavior was one of *tom*. In his developing human form, without being completely conscious, Wild Feather took *obedience* as a security blanket.

Wild Feather was a boy in a SURREAL-DREAM of which he could not wake from; he had to RIDE the apparent *Variable Mass* as it presented itself to him.

To his knowledge his mother was always on the bottle and never quite made sense when she spoke: at least not to a Native American boy of five living in a **forced-location**.

Wild Feather was a boy whose roots had been erased almost entirely by the new land owners. Invading-Entities who forced themselves onto the Americas at a time that was not Wild Feather's time but that of his ancestors.

In his current predicament, Wild Feather tried to find love in the men her mother brought home. Unfortunately there was no love (there was only the dire reality that he was not wanted and was seen by those frequent-visitors as *only-being-there*: of being some *Mishap* of their lover's past).

As Wild Feather stood, he decided to sit.

SIT

Since the dawn of the morning had not shone its elements, Wild Feather quickly rose from the ground...the Sting-of-the-Cold was instant and his body was not able to tolerate it. He stood up again quickly.

QUICKLY

Wild Feather decided to walk to keep warm.

He walked on the rocky ground and headed to nowhere; but for him it was somewhere away from that run-down one-bedroom house-shack where he often slept in the living room.

Wild Feather wanted something but was not able to comprehend what it was.

Wild Feather unconsciously sought the warmth-of-love but was unable to express it in thought due-to-the-fact that he had very little of love in his tiny-existence.

In Wild Feather's mind, he possessed an illusion that he felt for his mother and glimpses of a memory he had for his father.

A father he could not grasp...a father he never really knew a father that was dead.

DEAD

Wild Feather was already five and could not speak.

He had been a product-of-neglect ever since his mother became the local drunk.

The shack houses were far apart and he really had no friends to call his own. When her mother occasionally took him to the tiny Indian town, he found knick knacks here and there; but soon realized he could not have them.

Wild Feather never asked his mother for anything except for her love and affection. Although he was not conscious of it, Wild Feather knew his mother was poor. What he didn't realize, not even subconsciously, was that his mother spent what little they had of money mostly on alcohol.

For his mother, THE DRINK represented an *escape* and *comfort* from all her misfortunes that were brought upon her and those she brought upon herself.

Wild Feather walked and walked in the cold as if waiting to see something.

"waiting to see" [what what where]

...something that never materialized *not* even *in mind*.

Wild Feather became very cold and decided that it was best he turn back.

As he walked, he looked at the pieces-of-pebbles that littered the ground. He tried to find meaning in them and even tried to explore theories; but his capacity at that age was limited, especially since he-had-no-formal-nourishments to help him expand on his mind's questions.

The brief time he had with his mother on a non-alcoholic level was rare.

Mother was not there for him; she was depressed and in silence, just feeling sorry for herself.

Whenever Wild Feather attempted to verbalize questions he had about something her answer became like a broken-record. Mother announced THE SAME at-every-verbal-sound that came from her son's mouth: "Just go play outside".

If Wild Feather insisted, his mother would raise her voice and repeated THE SAME. Wild Feather quickly learned that she could not be reached. Mother was *not there* (although in body she was). She was somewhere else.

some   where   else

But like an innocent child: Wild Feather loved his mother dearly and unconditionally.... and dearly he sought her *affection* and attention.

affection and attention

affection and attention

Despite the obvious, Wild Feather never lost Hope never lost Faith in his mother.

He now and then tried to resuscitate his mother with his questions-of-observations in verbal sounds that had NO high-comprehensible-language.

This boy hesitated in his attempts to form words and phrases since he had NO consistent-verbal-models from which to reference.

This continued until he found her *dead* one morning at the age of *seven*.

Age-of-*Seven*

DEAD

Seven.

DEAD

The woman lay on the floor with her head down. "Mommi, mommi" Wild Feather spoke to her while he tugged at her arm.

The woman would not move.

Wild Feather had discovered his mother on the kitchen floor when he woke up that morning. The cold air entering his lungs while sleeping in a mat in the living room is what woke Wild Feather to this nightmare.

The five year old boy kept on tugging at his mother and began to feel a DREAD he had never felt before. "Mommi, mommi wake up mommi!"

He yelled at her.

Wild Feather sat down on the floor next to her: hoping that maybe she would wake.

Wild Feather did not want to believe his mother was dead like his dog had died one winter day from hunger.

The dog was nearly bare bones when it died. The child had no idea he had died of hunger. He was *six* minus 2 when his dog died *six* minus 2.

six minus 2

And now in his current misfortune a CORRELATION between his dead dog and his mother were beginning to formulate in his mind.

Wild Feather sat there.

He sat there.

He sat there.

Wild Feather had not gone to school all that time; his mother never cared to enroll him, and everyone was so separate that no one noticed his absence from school.

In fact, Wild Feather had never been registered at birth and really had no record of being in existence!

After a long pause on the kitchen floor, Wild Feather got up and tried to turn his mother.

Her hand was hidden inside her.

When he finally turned her, he saw that her gown was soaked in *blood*.

A knife was in her stomach being grasped with her clinched fist firmly around the handle.

Her *stare* was one of *sorrow*.

There was no expression of pain on her face: just *sorrow*.

so rrow

Her mouth was opened in an oval shape. Her teeth were not visible.

He yelled at her, "Mommi, mommi…why!?"

"Why mommi?!!".

Wild Feather knew then she had *gone* away for good. Worst of all, away from him! Now she had gone away in body as well.

Wild Feather sat near her and began to cry uncontrollably like he never had before.

He sobbed and sobbed and sobbed.

No one heard him.

He sobbed for about an hour until his body could *no longer sustain* the grief he felt inside.

Uncontrollable was his mind and he fell asleep.

In his dream, Wild Feather felt like all what had just happened was only a bad dream.

...an involuntary fantasy...a false protectionism-mechanism

ISM.

Wild Feather felt that he was in the living room sleeping and his mother in the room sleeping.

In his dream-sleep, the boy Wild Feather would soon go to her but felt like staying under his ragged sheets.

...He promised himself he would later go to her and ask her a question. He felt comfort in this reality he had created in his dream.

In This dream he had no idea what had happened. All he knew is that it was a bad-dream and he had awakened from it.

Unfortunately, after a WHILE, while in his dream, Wild Feather began to realize more and more and more that his mother was now gone from him.

The boy Wild Feather was now conscious in his dream and did not want to wake; not yet. He needed to gain enough strength before he woke to this horrific scene.

He kept his eyes closed.

Finally, Wild Feather felt it was time.

*Ggg*rasping the floor with his fingers; he began to apply pressure to the ground to lift himself from it.

When young Wild Feather stood, he *slowly* opened his eyes.

There was his mother.

...just as he had seen her before he slept.

He momentarily stood *over* her.

The boy Wild Feather then turned around and headed outside to the porch.

For *3 days* Wild Feather just stood or laid outside his house...a stern *cyclical Mercurialis*-jerky state of trauma had enslaved him.

ENSLAVED him.

It was as though the gods conspired against Wild Feather: with *Osiris* marking him for *extinction*.

The boy did not eat or drink and was getting weaker as the days-drew-near.

On the fourth day, one of his mother's boyfriends found him and the body. The *Ex-Lover* notified the local authorities.

Wild Feather survived if only in body.

The trauma BESTOWED-ON-HIM was not easily resolved: and this proved true in future relationships he had with women as he grew into a man.

Wild Feather had been in foster care at first until they found an aunt from his father's side that was willing to take him in.

She lived just outside of the Reservation.

Wild Feather recuperated somewhat since his aunt Tide-Water was loving.

She never married and lived alone.

Alone but Content.

Content.

With the help of "Tide-Water", Wild Feather was able to be social: even somewhat happy and outgoing.

As time went by, Wild Feather finished high school.

After this schooling, he began to look for work in the big city closest to the reservation.

Oklahoma City

homa   homa
homa   homa

After a bit of a struggle, Wild Feather found a job as a trash collector with the city. He got that job after applying a *dozen* times.

dozen

dozen

yes

dozen

dozen

Wild Feather was so annoyingly

annoyingly

annoyingly persistent that the city's maintenance manager finally gave him an opportunity when an opening came.

Wild Feather had appetizing facial and bodily features.

He stood at *six* feet *two* inches with a perfect muscular physique. He easily attracted *any* woman.

As time passed, he had relationships but never seemed to stick to *one*.

Wild Feather was careful if sexual intercourse was in the relationship...he did not want to bring any child into this world.

no child   no child   no no child

nonochild   child-no-no   child no!

He always wore condoms **or** sought abstinence.

Abstinence was difficult for the women who wanted him PURELY-for-the-PLEASURE.

The women he was with just COULD-NOT-RESIST him and INSISTED on consummating their loose relationships.

Although some of them pretended not to be in need....the pull was **SO STRONG** they had to stop lying to themselves, and to the object of their sexual desire: the boy who became a man:

Wild **F**eather.

The women's sexual hormones always went **hay-wire** when they *held* him....going completely OUT–OF–CONTROL!

O   U   T- O F - C   O N   *TROL !*

At times the negative side of Wild Feather would seek its revenge: he had the PERMANENT *scar* of his mother and would all of a sudden fall into a ho***rri***ble ho***rri***fic depression where he would lock himself in his room and not come out for days.

By an unknown *power*, he was always able to recuperate and pull himself out of his turmoil (a turmoil which included involuntary fasting **spiked-BY** the *absence* of water).

When a few of his girlfriends of a time, one at a time, were there, they couldn't understand his *being* when it came to these bouts-of SELF-IMPOSED-ISOLATION: those actions scared them.

The few unfortunate women that experienced this wanted to help him: but he would just close the door and not come out.

The male friends he had made k*new* this ran-**D**oom ritual and let him be. They would come around a couple of days during his isolations and attempted to talk him into coming back.

No one out of the reservation knew his past: he never shared intimate things to anyone.

His friends nonetheless knew *something* in his past had brought him to these **EXTREMES**. They genuinely loved him because Wild Feather was a loyal and trustworthy friend.

One day, his friend, Johnny Wilkinson urged him to seek a psychiatrist to help him during these troubled moments.

Wild Feather refused.

At the end his friends just let him be...these bouts-of-isolation were not common so they let the random occurrences run-their-course.

Most of the time, Wild Feather was happy and normal and would love to socialize till the morning hours with his buddies or spend time with his present girlfriend of a time.

Whenever one of his girlfriends asked for marriage, he would drop them with a sermon that he *couldn't'* continue with them and thanked them for giving him their love and care.

They insisted on staying; but, after knowing their intention, he made it clear that it was over by going up to them and telling them, *over* and *over*, "it's *over*"---until they had *no choice* but to walk away in sorrow and let him be.

These women had high hopes that he would call them back; but as the months became years, they moved on.

Chapter Twenty
Doris Withirt Ó Coileáin
(Jana's Mother)

Doris Withirt Ó Coileáin grew up a happy child up-to-the-death of her parents at the age of *twelve*.

Prior to her misfortune, Doris' parents and their few friends had plans to immigrate to **O**klahoma from **N**ew **Y**ork: and prior to that they had immigrated from **Ireland** in the early *nine*teen *fift*ies.

early   *nine*   teen   *fift*ies.

>**C**ontae Chorcaí, Ériu >>New York

>>> **O**klahoma
[got it!:)]

Doris' father, *Michael* Ó Coileáin *Jun*ior (named after his father) was known as "Gillby" since he was an avid swimmer. He spent hours-a-day swimming into anything that had water...even icy waters!

[Uuoooh cold cold agetsa time agetsa uesta iet! J:)]

军

Gillby had fought in the Great War of the 1940s as a volunteer in the British Army.

This was *un*USUAL considering that both Ireland and Britain had been *rival*s because of Britain's encroachment into Ireland lands in the past and present!

In fact, they still are *riva*ls!

In the first two decades of the 1900s, Michael's father was a STRONG advocate for independence of Ireland from British control.

That involvement got him killed...but not before he *stirred* the spirit of his fellow Irish.

Because of that murder: Gillby never had the opportunity to know his father. But, SOMEHOW

HOW HOW, he felt a deep connection to him; as if *telepathically*.

[no Not 'Pathetic'!!!]

Gillby was the "HIDDEN" child in order to protect him from mercenaries-of-the-British-Empire...who like most Empires, sought to destroy the resistance right down to the Last-Male-Child.

During the war, Gillby made many English friends as well as American friends. These non-national-patriots-for-freedom, at the beginning of the end of the war, joined the "Americans" at the Lion's Lair in Berlin for the last showdowns to spell "V i c t o r y" for a *theatre war* that used voluntary and involuntary real actors!

[Sí Ja Yes *"theatre war"* believe it!!!]

The price for this deceptive and *forced* admission into this *theatre war* spelled bodily death or emotional and psychological mental damage, and or loss of limb for many who voluntarily and involuntarily participated.

VOLUNTARY AND INVOLUNTARY

those who knew the lie were the voluntary; and those who believed in or didn't believe in or didn't care to get involved in the lie were involuntary.

[why all the fuss Mi'Kha-el? ...because we must remember the pain to understand our own decision making! Making Decisions! Decision Making!]

The deception was an ORCHESTRATION by all the governments that participated in that *theatre war* (and past and future wars): many faces but one agenda; many faces but one ruling entity; many faces but...you get the picture! A hidden agenda not even fathomed by the average Carbon Internato!

After the war, these *new* friends remained friends and kept in touch with each other. All those fighting for the cause suffered much and these *muc*h experiences created an unbreakable bound which kept them in close relations.

When Gillby returned to Ireland from the Great-2nd-War, he met Doris' mother in college where both pursued their education.

Doris' mother had a heart to help people and wanted to serve as did Gillby as teachers in the primary grades.

After graduation from **Coláiste na hO**llscoile, **Corcaigh**, both began to teach.

They did not consummate their relationship until after their marriage in 1949. Doris, Jana's mother, was conceived that year and was a happy child who smiled a lot. They loved her dearly.

When Doris was four, the Ó Coileáin family of three immigrated to America where a friend of Gillby had invited them to stay in New York. They had free accommodations until they found jobs and a place of their own to settle down.

New York during that time was vibrant and busy with money funneling in from *unknown* sources! Doris' mother brought her younger sister Betsy with her from Ireland.

Betsy was a young 25 year old with an adventurous spirit and was more than willing to get out of Ireland and join them in the *New World*!

Betsy met her husband Howard who was from Oklahoma. He was in New York on business and had met Betsy at a parlor. Both hit it up and soon married. Betsy soon after the wedding moved West to Oklahoma City to move in with her husband.

Back in the State of New York, after about 7 years working as teachers in the Bronx, the Ó Coileáin couple wanted a better environment for their daughter.

On Doris' twelfth birthday on June the 4th, the Ó Coileáin family decided to move to a quieter environment in Tulsa, Oklahoma.

During the times they had visited Betsy, they had grown to love the plains of Oklahoma and the quietness of the space that divided the people into *Catacombs-of-Silence.*

So on the 4th of June, as their car raced on the highway towards Oklahoma, smiles were on their faces...all were excited about starting a new life in a new place. It seems like they were tourists wanting more and more of the new!

Gillby, wife Caragh, and child Doris had left the Bronx in the late afternoon and intended on driving in the cool night to avoid heat and traffic.

Gillby had planned accordingly by sleeping until departure time.

He and his wife Caragh would rotate as drivers to make it less stressful on the body.

When the sunrise's *rose* came to a temporary fix in the planet's rotation, they had planned to rest at a motel for a few hours...showering and changing of clothes to feel refreshed.

While the couple slept at the Motel, Doris would work on her school homework or color in her coloring book or dance in cat like movements (in order not to wake her parents). Little Doris was also looking forward to watching a little bit of television at the motel if they had cart*oons*.

The couple's overall plan was first to arrive at Bet*sey*'s to acclimate themselves. After a week of rest, there furniture and other personal belongings were scheduled to arrive to their new house they had purchased in Tulsa. The couple had paid a shipping company to transport them a week after they were scheduled to arrive to Oklahoma.

Betsey had insisted that they come to her house first since she wanted to give them a warm meal when they arrived and a hearty breakfast. At first they were reluctant but then accepted the invitation. Caragh sensed that her younger sister needed "together time":

Sister to Sister.

After the sun had somewhat subsided, the family began their driving journey once more to Oklahoma.

At about *2* in the morning, the sky was *black* and littered with *stars*. Mrs. Ó Coileáin and Doris were sound asleep.

As Gillby drove he began to dose off and tried to stay awake. He began to struggle with his eyes and would cough lightly to try to keep himself awake.

Gillby didn't want to wake his passengers.

After a while, Gillby began to see a house and a clear-bright sky and a road different than that which the car was actually driving on!!!

Gillby began to *feel* at ease and *felt fine*.

Unawares, a sudden blare of sound came to his ears. Taking an *automatic* deep breath he woke.

Gillby realized immediately that the images of bright skies and a beautiful neighborhood were painted images in his dream and that he had been asleep.

The sound had come from a big rig that honked its horn at him since he was veering further off to the opposing traffic on the off-route road he had driven onto accidentally.

"What's going on" his wife yelled as she woke.

Doris slept despite all the commotion. She slept in the back seat of their 1950 Station Wagon.

This *rectangular* car was pulling a small size trailer with their immediate belongings.

Gillby struggled to convince himself that he could go on. He was in the middle of nowhere and did not want to pull over and sleep. He thought about asking his wife to take over the drive; but decided it was best to find the nearest town and find some lodgings.

Gillby told Mrs. Ó Coileáin that he would keep driving till he found lodging. She would stay up to help keep him awake.

As they drove ONWARD, the young Irish couple talked about their future and how they would find new friends and build additions to their newly acquired *3* acre lot in Tulsa. They wanted horses and pigs and chickens and wanted to grow crops of corn.

As they talked, there was an intersection or rather a perpendicular division on the road with two entering dirt roads...one on the left side one on the right side

one on the Left side ... one on the Right side...

(It lay about a mile ahead).

There was no sound; no indication of an impending *death*! Everything seemed fine as they conversed.

But, as fate would have it, [and it did!] all their developing plans were slowly fading into permanent *dwarfed* aspirations.

On that intersecting dirt road ahead on the Left side (about a mile in) ...an old pick-up truck was quickly approaching the intersection...that is, approaching the off-route main road the Ó Coileáin family were riding on.

The driver of this old truck went by the name of *Judd Non Più* .

Judd *had* been out drinking and *had* been at his friend's *Jethro*'s h*ouse*. He *had* been complaining about how his girlfriend would not see him no mo'; how he was so angry he wanted to hurt her. His emotions were mixed. He loved her but knew her love for him had gone under the bottle...unda da 'bol'...too difficult to grasp!

Judd's now ex-girlfriend had made up her mind to move on and look for love without the alcohol. The night before she had completely called it off with Judd: "Get the fuck out of my house!" "Don't you ever return or I will kill you!"

Judd was NOT a happy camper.

As he drove, completely intoxicated, and only being able to drive because it was the only narrow road home; a road that had in the past saved him many times from crashing: because every time he veered off right or left, the swellings before the side canal ditches at-the-side-ends of the dirt road always brought him to the middle of the road again allowing him to continue ONWARD.

But on that dramatic night-of-misjudgments for this **Dirt Rider**, Judd was not only excessively drunk but very upset.

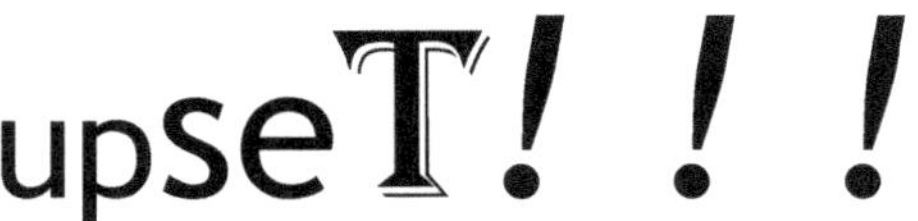

Judd felt the *swelling* of the dirt to the sides as he veered to one side of the road. He then decided (Out-Of-Anger) to violently get off the road but couldn't ...

Couldn'T! ! !

The road would not let him.

The road had a mind of its own and wanted to *saVe* Judd from his temporary emotional Bash!

This dirt-road had been dug about *two* feet under ground-level and then ELEVATED about *two* feet high to the sides...this elevation was made of packed dirt that came BEFORE the MAN-MADE-DITCH on the sides that were 6-feet-DEEP CANALS that ran on each side of the dirt road...it was made to divert water during the harsh rainy seasons.

Once this dirt road's 6-feet-DEEP side CANALS *N E A R E D* to about 6-feet from the off-route paved main highway, they IMMEDIATELY

ran-into a huge drain pipe that went underneath this main highway...diverting the water under and away from the main highway and then emerging on the other side where the canals continued

towards a **HUGE** crater -made -Lake.

On that night (of negative-emotions), Judd wanted to leave these dimensional-confines and feel free to move around.

His old Ford Pick-up truck was something he was tired of possessing as well.

If he were to remain in his body, Judd thought that maybe he wanted to be different: stop the drinking and maybe be more attentive to everyday issues: but Judd found it difficult to do either.

Back to his present with his hands on the wheel of this old beat-up truck, Judd drove with the head lights off.

He NEVER drove with the lights-on since he found no need for them. This road would continue until he would find the light **on** in-front-of-his-porch. It was as if he could see this guiding light for miles and miles ahead.

But that night his eyes were not on the light!

As Judd drove he became more and more agitated because of his *unresolves* and decided to **increase** his speed.

The odometer on his truck was past its capacity as he drove 150 miles an hour. His truck's engine seemed to struggle to maintain *that* speed.

Judd began to cry and this was unusual since he was not a *Crying Man*.

As fate had it planned, when Judd reached the main off-route paved highway, which he needed to cross to continue on the dirt road home, he **SLAMMED** his speeding truck **RIGHT-INTO-THE** Ó Coileáin's car that was about to pass the perpendicular inter**deception** (intersection).

The impact was extreme.

Judd broke the truck's windshield with his head and proceeded violently out while his lower body became *slicingly* stuck at the steering wheel and only a portion of him went out past the hood of the truck.

His *heart* began to slow as he exited the confines of his body not knowing where he was. Judd became a *confused bodiless energy*...not understanding anything but the programming he

had experienced when in his wretched body.

The Ó Coileáin's car was completely smashed in the side of the front driver seat and went flying.

flying

Mrs. Ó Coileáin, who was seated in the passenger side, began involuntarily banging her head violently (back and forth against the front passenger window): her skull cracked and began to bleed profusely. >>>> .... >>>> .... .>>>> ....

pro *fusely*

p r o f u s e l y

Unlike Gillby, she died a bit slower and could feel the pain... and finally she left her body.

Both cars tumbled to the side of the road and turned *twice seven* for the station wagon and its hitch, and *tetra seven f*or the truck.

The only survivor of the collision:

Doris.

Mrs. Ó Coileáin had created a circular "sofa" back seat with pillows and blankets for her daughter.

She had been thinking of ways to make it seem to Doris that she was in a cloud of comfort. Mother Caragh Ó Coileáin had thought of that idea before they began their trip.

So, not knowing the apparent positive consequences of her actions, Mrs. Ó Coileáin provided Doris a unique, safely snugged *egg*-like protectant around her daughter.

And although Doris did suffer some minor bangs and slight injuries to her body, her vital organs, including her head, had been preserved. And none of her bones were broken.

What Doris remembers is waking up to *a violent world* around her. Startled, she tried to sit up but was pushed back by the violent centrifugal force that moved around her.

In fact, it was *this force* that saved her; it was only toward the slowing of the vehicle that she began to bang herself to parts of the car that surrounded her.

When the vehicle finally halted, Doris lay back in her original position and cried out to her mother.

There was no answer.

Young twelve year-old Doris was dizzy.

"Dad" she cried out afterward.

No answer.

Young Doris began to cry CANOROUSLY with her isolated sentiments.

She felt completely alone.

Doris Ó Coileáin was alone.

...Alone from any *human* contact.

The cold air around her began to creep into her and Doris began to find it difficult to breathe.

Instinctively as to her body's needs she *submerged* her whole carbon back into the covers and laid quietly in them.

Doris was unable to think of nothing more than to survive.

Doris wanted to live!...but away from the deceit; as if part of her knew "*the condition*". It *D*id *K*now: but the *crafty encasement* was meant to deter memories coming from the un-encased part of her Eternal Energy; and so there was a *power struggle* in an undetectable frequency.

As she lay, young pre-teen Doris fell into sleep and began to dream.

Doris found herself in a *hole*; a tunnel of sorts. It was narrow and made completely of earth.

Doris found herself in a rabbit's hole!

She was barely able to move.

Doris had to crawl.

c r a w l l l

Doris began to feel claustrophobic which led her to a *state of panic*.

Her breaths were short as if the elements were leaving her!

Young Doris tried to regain the *oxy*-gène by rapid, automatic gasps of her lungs.

It was as though Doris had asthma...not enough oxygen was reaching the body...pains began to escalate in her encasement.

Antoine's combustible 8 was in short supply for the created prison (a machine created for the transformation of *E*ternal *E*nergy to feed the growing appetite of its maker; a plan of consumption was its end-objective!).

After 43 minutes of *painfull time*, young Doris heard a sound like that of a squealing raccoon. It began to get louder as if the *beast* were nearing.

Raccoons: the treacherous fearless mischievous intelligent rodents terrorizing their human counterparts! *!*   *!*

 The sound kept getting *louder* and ***louder*** and ***louder***...Doris' heart began racing!
...and the walls made of *earth* began to vibrate as if alive.

Sounds of the Beast kept getting *nearer* and *nearer* and *nearer*!

Twelve year old Doris opened her eyes and saw far far far away at the end of one end of the tunnel a *light.*

Her *body's inclinations* raced toward it!

As the light became brighter, Doris began to see nothing but *white* [a specially designed kneader of creation].

Doris needed to get out of this hole and tried pushing out the earth in order to reach the light (𝕰𝖆𝖗𝖙𝖍 weighing beyond what Doris could push).

Young Doris began to *scream.*

She couldn't take it anymore.

𝕾𝖈𝖗𝖊𝖆𝖒𝖘 became longer and Doris began to breathe **heavily**.

On her third deep breath Doris found a huge rubber mask around her. She opened her eyes again and this time Doris was on the floor and outside the wreckage.

A gurney was under her and about three paramedics surrounded her.

a b o u t

T H A R T   A R

"Can you hear us?" one shouted!

"Can you hear us!?"

Young Doris could not answer because she could not make out what the man was telling her.

It was as though *English* had been wiped from her mind; as though part of the *programming* had been stripped!

s   t   r   i   p
p   e   d   !

One of them clapped loudly with his hands in front of her face: no reaction!

Doris' breathing became faint and CPR began to be administered to her.

All that **deep** breathing was *in her mind*:

An Illusion...

IIILLL   LLLUUU   SSSIIIOOONNN

...maybe a desperate attempt by *the body* to help itself by pleading with the encased Eternal Energy...desperately trying to convince it to come back to the 𝔪aker's created ℜeality!

...maybe it was *the body* shooting out another *electrical signal of deception* wanting to convince Doris this creation was eternal.

But the actualities-of-T H I N G S were that Doris' heart pulse was *f*aint and *f*ading; the men rushed her into an awaiting ambulance and immediately gave her electric shocks to revive the fading heartbeat that had apparently stopped!

S T O P P E D !

S T O P P E D !

S T O P P E D !

At the third-fourth treatment, Twelve year old Doris reacted to her body's demand.

Doris stabilized into the encasement.

...but did not say a word.

Doris again closed the eyes and slept. This time, she did not *dream*.

Doris woke the next afternoon and saw that she was in a room with all these unknown monitors around her. Doris tried to move her arms but felt pain in them.

Doris had numerous IVs running in her veins, and monitors of sorts attached to her as well.

This child had been poked a **my**riad-**o**f-**t**imes in each limb *previously*: which left her with an abundance of bruised purplish marks on her arms and legs.

At times the nurses could not find reliable veins to place the IV or to draw blood for *apparent* needed analysis.

After several attempts during separate times, they reached adequate *gey*ser-ettes!

ettes! ettes!

Many times the nurses seemed incompetent [and many of them were!] with bursts of blood spilling {splattering} over her *white* sheets.

(*t*hey {artwork on white canvas} **were**:

quickly, Swiftly, Briskly, Doub-ly, Lickety-*Split-ly*, **Warp**sly, **Warp**-Sedly, ASAP-Sly, *C*epetly, Sugu *N*i-ly すばや, *D*engan *C*epat-ly, *T*ezlik *B*ilan-ly, N*G*okushesha-ly

*A*ND

quietly, iNaudibly, Tacitus-ly, ThegJa-sly, **TYST**-ly, **SeK**in-ly, *L*eise-ly, *Y*n *D*awel-ly ...

i-mmed-iate-ly

removed*.*

...no traces of error could be found except those obvious ones left on her limbs).

Doris, An Maighdean Óg, could not speak for some odd reason.

The doctors communicated with her when they came in each morning.

Doris would nod a yes and a no to answer their questions.

It was not until the *seventh* day that some sort of fuzzy speech came out of her mouth.

Doris tried hard to make words but found her tongue *unwilling*.

The hospital sent in a speech therapist that worked with her tongue muscles: doing all sorts of exercises.

[exercise good J. Yes J:)]

On the twelfth day, young Doris was able to speak and had gained her confidence that everything was going to be alright for her.

This incoming, regular influx of speech may have been initiated when one of the doctors finally told her the night before (on the 11th night at the hospital) as a confirmation of:

```
what-had-happened.
```

And, even though Doris had not inquired about it the many days prior, she knew that her parents were *dead*.

Their confirmation did not do *ANYTHING* to her for Doris had been crying (silently and painfully) every day (silently and painfully) since that afternoon (silently and painfully) when she had *awoken* from her deep sleep: knowing exactly what that silence meant that dreadful night.

pain, silence, dread, anguish, despair, suffocating, dizziness, no return, no esperanza for their beautiful bodies to embrace her again.

The again had died.

The again had died.

The again had died.

"silently and painfully" Doris endured her pain at that hospital.

Doris had to be strong!!!

...something inside her compelled her to move on!!!

...to say goodbye in her heart to "Máthair Caragh agus Athair Gillby":

"Is breá liom tú araon i gcónaí!"

..."Mhúin tú dom a bheith láidir!" ..."Chun mo chuid mothúchán a rialú!"

..."Buaileamar le chéile arís mo thuismitheoirí álainn lá amháin!"

Her aunt Betsy had been informed but found it troubling (among other things) to be with a child that had gone through such a horrific incident.

Betsy's flare since her arrival to the Americas to *extinguish* all negative thoughts from her mind had faded *unwillingly*.

Betsy now was an obscure being who (propelled by her husband's *hidden* manic depression) deliberately alienated herself from anything that would bring negative emotions to her being. Betsy tolerated her husband since she *knew* no-way-out!

In fact, when the social services approached her and asked her to take custody of young Doris, Betsy hesitated and was dreadful all-inside-her-being: quietly not expressing the DREAD inside.

That is probably why Doris' mother had a hunch that her sister needed her...and indeed that was the case.

Because of their dramatic hidden-past traumas respectively, Betsy and *her* husband *had* decided long ago that they would have no children of their own. They wanted to salvage what comfort zone they had to themselves...believing that a newborn just spelled T R O U B L E

T R O U B L E
        T R O U B L E

This **hysteria** that affected this unusual couple into mental anguish and manifested physical ailment was mind boggling...

boggling mind mind mind mind!

...and to have a mania about rejecting all "minors" was not too explicable since their home in Tulsa was *quietly*-situated in a peaceful neighborhood inviting children in!

c h i l d ren i n!

mania **hysteria hysteria** mania...

.... described this Oklahoma couple to a definitive precision....a very unfortunate if Doris enters there home to live there!

There was something about this household that didn't seem right.

[like most households of the world, unfortunately!]

The social worker asked Betsy to think about it and encouraged her to take Doris in since the other alternative was foster care.

Betsy was given a week to think about it so that a decision would coincide with the date Doris would be ready to be released from the hospital.

released from the hospital **released** from the hospital **released** from the hospital.

Betsy was perplexed.

...perplexion ran all over her mind like *confused ants* seeking to gain order in rank and file.

...this perplexion did not leave Betsy to a peaceful conclusion. And Howard was just depressed...things at work did not seem to be going smoothly...and coming home seemed like an arduous task!

TASK TASK TASK!

ARDUOUS!!!

ARDUOUS!

In her mind Betsy kept reversing herself at each

moment...misfires-of-**neurons** seemed

completely normal at this point for Betsy. She
wanted to be responsible and take her sister's
child in but was conflicted at the sheer notion of
taking in a girl that would soon hit puberty!

Multiple Reasons Not to Take young Doris in
were Created during the seven day deadline in
Betsy's head!

head head Betsy

COMPLETELY Wacked!

...Coupling **DAT** with her doubts: Betsey did not
trust her husband who became more and more
depressed as the days grew. [how can days grow?
Good question.]

Betsy had tried everything to make Howard happier but the pressures of his work at the local tire company had him on the edge

E D G E   E D G E *!!!*

Howard needed to make large sales quotas each week and he was unable to relax.

And Betsy was in denial...not realizing her craziness!

...taxīng taxīng taxīng on Howard's mind coming home became a nightmare!!!

With all that CRAP at home and at work how could Howard relax???!!!!!!! [ah]

...It was as though Howard knew no-other-way but to continue with a system of greed he had known all his life.

a l l   h i s   l i f e

And that greed led to deep depression!!!!

Howard was afraid to try something new.

Howard, like most "nation" North Americans and Europeans, including all those around the world, were\are **INFESTED** with the Western economically created idea, whole-heartedly believed in the newly formed slavery system they called Capitalism:

low wages for most and high wages for some:...and those in the middle...well, just temporary positioning! At the end, irrespectively, all ultimately suffer from burn-outs!..of being physically, psychologically, emotionally and spiritually pulled from normalcy, into chaotic schedules and routines! Intense Exploitation was/is key to those that run the "kill show"!!!!:(

An economic system which by design requires an EXORBITANT consumption of a human beings' precious time: **STRATEGICALLY** subtracting (on a second by second basis) the time desperately needed for a person's personal development in order to remember who they really are/ where they are/ and why they are truly here on this planet.

An ECONOMIC SYSTEM imposed on the entire world after the so called "Industrial Revolution" commenced in Europe in the late 1700's....Evidence that the British Empire STILL controls the so called "United States of America" nation!...it is done in secret! And who controls the B.E.? [good question…the Red Mad Hatters!!!]

....A transformation system from SLAVERY **TO** INDIRECT–HIDDEN SLAVERY to another variation soon to come!

…but like DUMB-ASSESS we we continue to accept this path of malignant evil disease!

DISEASE MALIGNANT MALIGNANT DISEASE!

The people of the world so naively believe that their government is for their overall well-being:

a lie.
lie
lie

lie!

A singular hidden, evil world government who controls all governments and trade by conglomerate corporations of the Rockefellers et al.—all Jewish corporations guised as Christians and other ridiculous denominations of beliefs that follow a "hidden" god who ultimately is that of the first major civilization god in Egypt...the God of Gods in their feeble minds.

Ancient Egyptian Hegemony still controls the world under the guise of governments and nations and religions. The evolution of disguises persists while their plan continues as they serve the 2nd Beast!...putting all humanity at risk!!!

No one (or at least most) knew or know how deep the deceit had dug itself in [in U !]:

...from created languages (English currently at its forefront) to the varied controlling cultures of the world to the "sciences" given to the public...all in an attempt to distract [**and they are succeeding**] and to hide their *true motive*.

…Follow the cookie crumbs to see what I say is true! Use your eternal mind! Connect with God the Father and the answers will pour!!!!

            … … …. …. …. …. …

Back to the present of Betsy's reality, the social worker made a tender offer to Betsy by offering a monthly some of money from the state-government if she took Doris in; in addition to the attractive attachment of the sale of Doris' parents' home they had just acquired, and savings to her name, made it more and more appealing to say 'yes'.

The verdict was in:

YES!$ $$

Betsy and her husband agreed to care for Doris.

As expected, Betsy cared for Doris' bodily needs but offered no affection of love.

Betsy showed Doris her room and instructed her that lights would be out at 9 p.m. every night and that she was not allowed to leave her room after that time except to use the bathroom once.

Doris tried to show affection to her aunt but Betsy was too involved in trying to please her husband... who simply became worse as the days grew nearer.

[How can 'days' grow 'nearer'?! Good question J:]

The **PSYCHO BOMB** to Betsy's husband Howard came about 2 years later one morning.

Howard was arriving at his office when he noticed that all his possessions were in boxes!

B O X E S ! ! !

The owner had decided to close shop and move on.

"Things happen Howie...sorry to let you go...but I'll be filing for personal bankruptcy tomorrow morning. I have more losses than gains for the past 6 months."

"Competition is fierce!"

"I had to borrow on our profits to pay for my personal expenses which included several mortgages..."

"And...I was gonna"

Howard for the first time in his human life was out of work!

OUT OF WORK!!!

After that troublesome morning of being fired, Howard tried looking for work but found none.

No one seemed to want to be associated with *anyone* who had worked at that tire company.

As a result Howard spent long hours at home **ALONE** (while Betsy went off to her new job as a waitress at the local diner).

Betsy's hours were reasonable at first (she would get home by six in the evening). But soon the welcoming committee had disappeared and her hours were changed to a `graveyard shift:`

...that started at 5 five **FIVE** in the AFTERNOON to THREE 3 **3** and sometimes FOUR 4 **4** in the MORNING!

As a result, she saw less and less of anyone at home.

Howard at first just hid himself in his room. His ritual was to lie on the floor in a curled position and just feel sorry for himself at his **inability** to get work.

inability

i n a b i l i t y

9   *9*   *9*

He had refused to see any doctors especially since he had no money to pay for one. Repetitively he had tried and tried to encourage himself by trying different sorts of ways to find work but nothing materialized.

Howard felt *cursed*!!!

cursed!!!

One night, while the **newly turned fourteen-year-old**-Doris was making a sandwich in the kitchen, she heard whimpering coming from Betsy's and Howard's room.

Doris knew Howard had issues but never dared to try to help.

But on that night, a month after Betsy's new changed work schedule had reached its MONTHIVERSARY, young Doris decided to knock at the door of the odd-couple's room.

"Howard! It's me: Doris. Open up".

Doris could hear Howard whimpering.

The young woman waited about 9 minutes when finally the door opened.

There stood Howard in tears.

He was six feet two inches tall.

"Come out to the living room. I want to talk to you." The young woman told him from outside the room.

Howard hesitated.

Doris then demanded, "Come on Howard!"

Howard attempted to leave the room but it was as though the door had some sort of magnetic field that repelled him back into the room.

MAGNETIC FIELD

Doris reached in and grabbed his hand and pulled him out-into the living room.

Doris sat him down on a lazy boy chair and pulled up a chair and sat next to him.

The young woman began:

"Listen, I know you are going through rough times not having a job and all."

"But life will get better."

"You will eventually find work and you will move on."

"Now, I don't know your history."

"But what I do remember when my parents and I came down to visit you one summer, back when I was very young, that you were a happy man."

"A Happy Man!"

"A very Hopeful Man!"

"Now, it is true you had money flowing in and your job was secure. But now you must *fight* to be positive. You must fight to get those negative feeling o u t of you!"

"*O u t of you!*"

"It won't be easy but it is *not* impossible."

Howard was amazed at what he heard coming out of Doris' mouth.

Howard began feeling hopeful.

It was as though Doris propelled magical words that were *un-kneading* the imperfections within Howard.

.....imperfections that he had not created, but rather imperfections that had unknowingly manifested themselves within his body (his encasement).

"Not all is gone Howard."

"You have your home, you have your wife, and you have me."

The young woman reached out and held his hand. Howard pressed his hand onto hers.

Howard spoke as if reviving and disinfecting himself from some-sort of
WITCHCRAFT!

WitchCraft!

"Doris you *truly* have words of wisdom beyond your years. It is hard for me to change the dreadfulness I feel inside; I feel like I'm useless; like incompetent; like not knowing or having direction".

"But what you say is *true*." Howard continued.

"I must break this cycle of dread. Even lately I've thought of ending it all."

Howard went on and spoke as young Doris sat and listened to him.

What Betsy could not do (listen and offer clear advice) Doris offered and gave freely and unpretentiously.

Betsy was not the educated kind, or the kind that could even have patience to sit for a while and listen to grievances or offer advice. Betsy was always TOO-wound-up in her fantasies or wants...not being able to see *beyond* her "programmed" human-self.

Even when Betsy tried to be different, her human genetic makeup was **TOO STRONG**. Frankly, [hey Frank!], it was a monumental struggle for Betsy to offer her husband competent-nurturing help he desperately needed at this point in his life.

It takes a *being* within such an encasement (the human biological encasement) *much* discipline and realization to overcome the programming, to go beyond the barriers, in order to **see** clearly and to **act** clearly...both essential…to competently help another:

SEE and **ACT!**

Little by little, as the days past, Howard began to improve like never before!

As often as possible, Doris would sit with Howard. Howard would go over his anguishes from childhood to the present.

The young woman listened as Howard spoke.

The young woman listened as Howard spoke.

The young woman listened as Howard spoke.

The sessions became "unofficial" therapy sessions where the patient was able to find the *light* through the expression of spoken words.

s   p   o   k   e   n   w   o   r   d   s

Although Doris was too young to give him any practical advice, she did however provide what Howard needed: an ear and a nod of understanding.

AN EAR AND A NOD OF UNDER STANDING

…someone to convey emotions, confusions, and aspirations!

…someone who would not judge just listen.

…not judge just listen

…not judge just listen.

As the days became weeks Howard became stronger!

S T R O N GER!

Gradually Betsy became jealous of Doris. Betsy began to feel that maybe Doris was having an affair with Howard.

Consequently, Betsy grew a grudge against Doris.

GREW A **GRUDGE**

G R U D G E

Now, instead of just being non-emotional in not providing emotional expression of love toward Doris, Betsy found every excuse to verbally attack Doris for little things like leaving water on the bathroom floor after she had taken her bath.

Howard was not aware of the hostility because Betsy was very discreet about it.

In fact, the time came when Howard found work and was off and running again!

...but this time with a different mind-set*!!!!!!!*

It was not until Howard got total control of his life that Betsy finally was able to leave her job.

... but Betsy did not want to leave her job.

Betsy wanted to work.

Howard pleaded with Betsy to leave her job saying that he appreciated her big help financially when he lost his job, but insisted to her that he was now able to completely provide for the family without her having to work.

Betsy insisted though that she needed to work, she needed an outlet from the monotony.

Howard conceded and understood.

In an attempt to create a new environment for the family, Howard re-initiated his romanticism toward Betsy…something he had only done when they dated.

Howard began to do all sorts of romantic gestures like bringing her flowers after work, and bringing breakfast to Betsy on her days off.

Betsy was however cautious.

Betsy was hurt in her mind thinking that Howard and Doris were having an affair.

They were *so* friendly with each other that Betsy could not understand that it was *only* friendship.

O   N   L   Y   f r i e n d s h i p

One Saturday morning, Betsy heard Howard and Doris laughing about a joke Howard had learned at work.

Both were laughing from the top of their lungs and holding hands to try to control the uncontrollable laugh.

When Betsy came out from the bedroom she "caught them" holding hands and thought the worst.

"What are you both doing holding hands, eh!"

"What kind of mischief is going on here?"

Betsy continued *yelling*:

"What, what, what in hell is going on here?!!!"

Betsy then (for the first time) physically lashed out at Doris with both hands.

Doris fell to the ground as Betsy continued to rush toward her to pound her angers and frustrations at young Doris.

Howard immediately pulled Betsy away from her.

"What are you doing Bet! Leave her alone! Control yourself!"

Betsy then directed her attack on Howard:

"You unfaithful son of a bitch; I'm not your foul; your idiot; you thinkless asshole."

"CAC AR OINEACH!"

She attempted to hurt Howard.

"CIACH ORT!"

She did everything possible to slap him!

"TÉIGH TRAS *NA* O *RT* FÉIN "

She slapped Howard.

"Pian tú ar an asall!"

Betsy continued violently vibrating her hands at Howard...he quickly grabbed them and held them.

"What are you saying? What are you saying!?"

Betsy pushed herself away from Howard:

"You both are having an affair!!! You both are traitors!!!"

"**Traitors** I say!!!"

" **Traitors!! Traitors!!!** "

Howard responded:

"Are you out of your mind? She is just a girl!"

Betsy was in a frenzy and almost completely off-the-wall.

"You are my heart! I'm yours Bet!"

As Howard drew himself close to Betsy...the furious lioness was able to come-down-her-fury mountain and began to reason.

From that day forward, all the way up to when Doris met Wild Feather at seventeen, Howard had to cut his regular talks with Doris because of Betsy's jealousy.

The house became silent but Doris knew she had helped Howard with his issues.

Howard never returned to the *sorry state* he was in.

He became a positive being at every negative point that presented itself. Howard was able to rebound from ***demon*** attacks immediately!

Howard knew their *game* now!

...knowing they can use any physical vessel including his own encasement to cause him to doubt his true nature.

More and more Howard understood his *"Condition"* and meditated daily to connect to his eternal self...making a clear distinction between his encasement and what he really is:

an Eternal Being **trapped** in this *Creation* (but not eternally!)

Creation ...the human body, the other animal bodies, the plants, the world, the universes!

Doris, for her part, focused on school.

Doris began making plans to eventually move out after high school.

On-the-day she met Wild Feather, Doris had been asking the divine beings or God or gods to help her find someone she could *love* after she completed her post-high-school studies.

Boys at her school presented themselves with eagerness to young Doris: but Doris did not want to mix school with boys.

And so she told them, "let's be friends!..... but no more".

Many left broken hearted.

Others left with their unfulfilled-and-frustrated sexual needs!...getting a HARD-ON and having to beat off at *a fantasy* that wou'd-remain *a fantasy*!:(

Or could it be that their created fantasy (created Existence) is in fact just as valid as the experience they have in this world...in this world? Good question J.

J

On the streets men looked at Doris but they seemed disingenuous to her.

Of course, they just want to FUCK FUCK FUCK...... FUCK anything they could FUCK!

Hormones Remember...we are prisoners to the hormones!

Captives Yup!

And-in-the-event these Street Males did not get lucky (which is most of the time) they *AT LEAST* could take with them a pleasant *image* they could BEAT-OFF-TO at home!

In analysis of the preceding: everything in *this Creation* is just *electrical signals* anyway; so the beat-off is not a short-coming; in fact, they could create better *rendezvous* in their created existences...where they have more control*... than having to deal with all the shit of an unknown woman or man in this credulous world!

CREDULOUS WORLD

¿Sí o No? ¡Pues sí mamito! ¡No mames way!:)

That is, not having to deal with the consequences of a choice made by the penis or the clitoris! (both one in the same!)

CREDULOUS WORLD

*just as Satan has more control in this world...its created world. J

Chapter 21
*W*ild *F*eather *M*eets *J*ana's *M*other

At the age of *t* ·*wen* ·*ty fi·Vé*, while at a *C*ircle *K*, Wild Feather met Jana's mother who was buying a pastry as she walked to school. She was a beautiful young woman of seventeen. She was in her senior year of high school and had high hopes for the future.

She wanted to be a doctor and help people. She was determined to continue on this path, staying away from boys.

This *f*rame-*o*f-*m*ind worked until she saw Wild Feather.

She was immediately captivated by him as she pretended to turn around to look for milk just to see him.

There he stood: tall and handsome...brandishing a distinguished look as he pondered around the store trying to make up his mind on what to eat for breakfast.

It was 7:30 in the morning.

Wild Feather did not even notice her; maybe because he was *too-into-thought* about what to choose. That was very much like him; when he focused on something, everything else seemed to fade away.

Jana's mother tried to catch his attention by walking by him.

That didn't work.

She then decided it was best to ask him a question.

"Excuse me: do you know what time it is?"

She had to repeat it again until he finally noticed her.

"What is it you're asking?"

He looked down to where the voice came from.

There he saw a young girl with the *sweetest* smile.

She stood *five* feet *four* inches from the ground; and even though she was only *seventeen*, her body was formed to *per**fec**tion* as that of a full grown woman.

[the system made although in face usable is unusable as to its true intent. Also, Hamming is a willing pawn... like most Technologists, like Gates, are covers to something already there.]

Her breasts were formed into a *C* and her figure was slim and buttocks stood out with honors.

fec

*[a fraud by the face Administration; a **garble of lies** set to keep the deceit moving]*

She was one gal that any male would look at *intent-ly*.

But even with this, Wild Feather was not impressed...beauty in his eyes became complete with inner qualities that healthily *competed*

against the *V*isual.

He sought the *inner* beauty.......maybe because he thought that *in that way* he would be understood.

What drew his energies towards this young person was her honesty:

"Listen, my name is Doris, I'm going to be eighteen this June 4th, the month I graduate from high school. I saw you and I think you are beautiful."

"wow!" he thought.

She continued:

"I wanted to see you closer and here I am in your presence."

What courage!

What a demand to be acknowledged!

What un-cult-*Ural*-ly refreshing*!!!*

Wild Feather *immediately* fell for her.

Doris was like no other he had *ever* met.

He introduced himself with a name that she had never heard before. He said he was from the

Comanche descendants and lived in the city working as a garbage collector.

With not much in common between them at that moment except *their* honesty (at least that was what it seemed to be during this *first* encounter), a mutual *attraction* nevertheless was evident.

They both agreed to meet this Saturday at Circle K at 10 a.m. for a stroll around town in his pick-up truck; and lunch afterward.

Both were excited!.....each one could see this from the other's face as they departed company!

An Aurora eclipsed them by their hormonal bindings.

As they became Alone, both were so eager to see each other again. It was barely Moonday and each one felt it took, in their minds, an *eternity* for *Saturn*day to come on by.

But Ushas, Eos, and Newet kept them safe during each other's absence.....not allowing the interference by any programs as to what they both wanted...to be together.

They held together a bond destined for a ladder to a new beginning.....a *reversal of NOI-TA-ERC.*

An Occurrence ending the rebellion...tossing time and all the other programmings to the *Belter Smelter*: adding to the cleansing already in progress.

It would appear that the rebels had an infiltration amongst its ranks: yes, the rebels' scheme was never allowed to be permanent; a burst *without sever.*

When the day `finally` came for Doris and Wild Feather:

Romance was in the **A**ir!

With very few spoken words they both greeted each other about a

half an h**O U R** ear lier*!*

[OH MY J!!!]

Both had arrived earlier with great enthusiasm to please the other. It was as though they both sought

to prepare themselves for the servitude to
something that (both felt) **COMPLETED** them.

Wild Feather had never felt so much attraction to
'*N-ee* woman; he felt he had found his soul mate;
he felt he could tell Doris e-*vry*'-thing.

And he did.

Doris listened and offered her arms as comfort
when the sharing became difficult to *bear*.

BEAR

They talked for about 3 hours in his pickup truck.

He kept the engine running to keep the heat in the
truck working; it was about *35* degrees Fahrenheit
outside.

Wild Feather leaned forward and lowered his
head...he had a strong desire to kiss Doris.

Doris reciprocated by riSing to meet Wild
Feather.

The juices-of-LUBHYATI were rising!

The first kiss was slow and warm and wet and loving.

[4 rare adjectives in English: impressive:)]

4

küssen represented a biological bonding that sought a manifestation to their true nature.....of which memory was diverted from them; b *ut* the ultra-frequencies beyond dat of lengths of Gamma and Radio-although not known to public science: exist: and thus could not be channeled.....allowing them to keep their mutual desire to be eternally *one* to-the-other.

Both embraced each other and neither wanted to let go OR for the kiss to *e n d.*

The *Eight Ball* had not been dropped and the passion continued!

Both hugged One-Another and both felt a **security** they had never felt before.

In their beings a huge sigh of relieve revealed itself and they felt it run down from their heads to their toes to the ends of their fingers. Each gave a big long sigh of breath and began to breathe *s l o w l y.*

Their embrace seemed to synchronize their heart beats into one!

O n e

After a while they both decided to get breakfast for lunch at a local diner where they ordered the usual morning-American-meal: pancakes, eggs, sausage, and bacon.

To mark the special occasion, Wild Feather ordered a large fruit salad for them as well.

Now, in these types of establishments, their fruit salads were weak and small; so Wild Feather described to the waitress what he wanted and insisted that they use fresh, cut fruit, not the cans.

NOT THE CANS!

The waitress said it would cost substantially more for that side order. "I understand.",replied Wild Feather.

The owner, who was serving coffee to customers right next to them, overheard and nodded "yes" to the waitress.

The owner had never thought of doing something like that; would customers actually buy fresh cut fruit salad? It sounded like a good idea to *add* it to the basic menu.

The owner, in his late thirties, was the new owner of this roadside establishment. He had acquired the business from his grandfather. For him customer service was primordi-al[español] and he wanted to please this young couple: one of which consisted of a strong looking man with a stern face of determination, and the other a lovely *pink rose*!

Prime was on this young owner's mind!

The owner quickly took off his black apron and exited the small structure through the back door. He jumped into his pick-up truck and headed to the super market:

seven miles away.

SIETE

SIEBEN

In the new owner's thoughts, he had a *hunch* that such a treat would be a seller, even if it was priced above the usual dishes. Days later in the future he began to show case this fruit dish on the menu. *Lo[**Ki**]* and ***Be**hold*, it became a seller! *Jötnar* began to materialize itself and the diner was later to be called:

Jötnar Diner
HOME FOR THE GIANT APPETITES!

On that day though, the diner, owned by *Loki*, who worked indirectly with new beginnings, had not yet materialized into its future growths.

And there sat Wild Feather and Doris, waiting for their *order*.

It really wasn't a wait for them: it was an opportunity to *breathe* each-other-in...

...to contemplate the

"beings-in-possibilities".

Cont*end*ment existed in *that* diner on *that* day!

Wild Feather was happy!; Doris was happy!

Hec! Even the owner of the diner was happy!!!

Happy! Happy!

Երջանիկ

খুশি

*con*ten *tos*

Yerja*nik* Khu*śi*

JOY*EUX* *ha*_{ri} NA*tutu*^{WA}

*sáS*_{ta}

T S A S U*wan*d*e*

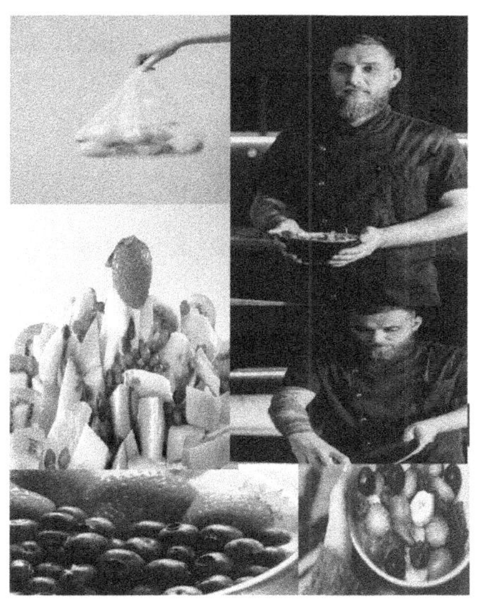

Chapter Twenty Two
Doris and Wild Feather
-A Wondrous Romance Unfolds-

Doris wanted someone who caught her attention right off the bat.

This someone was Wild Feather.

Never before had she seen such a man with a great physique: tall, dark, and handsome.

Seventeen year-old Doris was immediately interested in Wild Feather at the *CIR-C*le *K* where she laid her eyes on him for the *very* first *time*.

And, as it turned out the attraction was mutual...something beyond the physical.

Both spent as much time as possible with each other.

Wild Feather's emotional unstableness subsided at the hands of Doris who was very outspoken and caring.

Both felt a calmness with each other.

Both saw a future together.

The alignment of the stars had **NOT** planned this!

[This was a union for the purpose to *end* the rebellion!]

One day, Doris had had enough of Betsy who became increasingly daring in wanting to physically hurt her.

On that final straw day for Doris the ordeal was over a plate left unclean overnight. It was early in the morning hours, the night before prom-night on June 2nd, 1968.

Betsy had just arrived from her grave-yard shift and instantly became furious in the kitchen.

Betsy walked into Doris' room around 4 in the morning and *violently* pulled-Doris-out of her *sleep!*

Doris fell to the ground.

The next seconds that *tumbled* over consisted of insult after insult with Betsy *violently* waving her hands at Doris as if menacing slugs to her body.

Doris had not contemplated *as-of-that-date* in defending herself physically against a relative: especially her mother's sister.

In fact, Betsy was the *only* relative she ever knew!

But on that night, Doris' *peace* was beginning to *melt away* and her bodily temperatures were beginning to rise.

Howard was asleep and not aware of what was developing in the house.

Doris, who was turning eighteen (in two days!) became upset. For the first time in her five years living with Betsy, Doris *sprang*-off-the-ground and pushed Betsy back with both hands sending her against the wall.

"That is enough!!!"

Doris *sternly* told Betsy.

Betsy was startled at the reaction. The Perpetrator immediately stormed out of Doris' room in a *mixture* of fury and timidness.

Doris sat on the floor and began to cry.

She could not take Betsy's behavior any longer.

Doris had already applied to OSU (Oklahoma State University) who had accepted to admit her in the fall. Room and board were offered to her in the Oklahoma City campus.

THE FALL!!! .....the unhealthy circumstances made it unbearable for Doris to wait for the fall: Doris had to make a move now.

The 5th Year with Betsy had elon*gat*ed into an eternal S*pin* for Doris in her fragile young mind.

Doris packed her clothes, books, and other belongings and, after cleaning the dish she had left unwashed in the sink, went out of the house with one of her bags.

Doris walked in the cold dark to the local diner which was about a quarter of a mile away. It was *five-o'-five* in the morning when she arrived at the diner.

Placing her bag in a booth, Doris headed to the public-coin-telephone (which was just to the side near the bathroom stalls).

Doris dialed Wild Feather who was about to leave to work.

Wild Feather had heard of Doris' issues at home.

It was now arranged that he would pick up Doris, and then help her get her remaining belongings from Betsy's home in order to move out that very day.

Doris was relieved to have this love in her life who seemed to understand what she was going through.

After picking up the last of her belongings from Betsy's and Howard's home, Wild Feather drove her to his apartment. When they entered his home he told his love:

"This is your home now. Feel comfortable. There is plenty of food in the refrigerator and in the cabinets. I will see you at 3 when I return."

Wild Feather kissed Doris lightly on the forehead and *left*.

The apartment building was in an isolated part of Tulsa with run-down paint on the outside. There were only three-other-units in the building on the lot: making it easily accessible.

Doris felt safe and happy to be away from the *ILL-Tantalizing* Betsy.

Doris' *feelings* for Wild Feather were on the increase. And it seemed to her that her emotions were getting the best of her.

In the past, Doris always made it a point to let her analytical-self take control in making big decisions in her life: but at that moment it seemed *the emotions* were **edging** at being the DOMINANT-ONE in her decision-making of the present!

Being in his apartment at that very moment made her feel FREE, BEAUTIFUL, and LOVED.

LOVED she felt BEAUTIFUL she felt FREE she felt!

F   R   E   E   !

B E A U T I <u>F U L L</u>!

L O V E *D!*

Doris missed her mom and dad immensely up to the present (even though she made it a point to move on).

"Some things you can't deny," young Doris said to herself...understanding that as the years passed... attempting to **𝔴𝔥𝔦𝔰𝔨-𝔞𝔴𝔞𝔶** to OBLIVION the memories of those that had loved her immensely was not a choice.

NOT A CHOICE

It had now been a little over five years and Doris

s-t-*i-l-l* missed her parents with the **same-intensity** since the moment she lost them. A longing that *refuse*d to recede.

A l o n g i n g that *refuse*d to re*cede*.

The struggles not to leave those emotions behind kept on taunting for an audience (but what could Doris do?).

The lack of love of Betsy's made it difficult **not -to -long** for love...any-type-of-love!!!

But Doris Now had the Love-of-Her-Life to love...a being of beauty from the Comanche peoples!

The prom was on for that night and Doris had had h-i-g-h hopes of going and dancing. But now it seemed that maybe she shouldn't go.

Wild Feather arrived at 2:30 in the afternoon; he had left a bit early from work to see Doris.

Wild Feather loved Doris.

Yet this young lad was even conflicted with loving Doris…his past etched at him like a roaring lion trying to devour what good came his way.

The young Comanche feared that he might slip into those past destructive moods that dragged him away from people that loved him.

Wild Feather had major psychological issues that had *not* been completely addressed or resolved.

He knew that and feared it.

In an attempt to drown out those issues in the past from his head (which had been with him since childhood), Wild Feather often worked-hard-and-played-hard!

It was obvious to the *keen* observer that his troubled past subconsciously kept him in a state of emotional imbalance, producing unpredictability that could result in damage.

WHEN-A Frenzi*A*-M**ani***A* hit him as to this imbalance, boy turned man unsuccessfully tried to recover from them quickly; but was unable to pick himself up again without a good amount of time passing.

Wild Feather had to *wait* till the emotions subsided somehow.

As Wild Feather walked through the door, Doris received him with a kiss and **A STRONG AND L O N G** and gentle hug. [strong and gentle?! hmmmm.]

Sentiments poured out from Doris....she was vibrating out all those emotions of need for attention and peace.

Wild Feather received them with delight.

He immediately picked her up and h*eld*-her-tight.

They embraced and kissed for a long time. Then Wild Feather gently brought her down to an *old*, long sofa he had in the living room.

That moment became *intense* as Doris lay there receiving his body on top of hers.

Doris reached to unbutton his pants...but Wild Feather pulled away saying:

 "Sweetheart, your *P.R.O.M.*!"

"Let's get you ready for it." Wild Feather suggested.

Doris found it DIFFICULT to pull away. She wanted him *SOOO*-badly:

Doris' reproductive organs were *crying*-for-Wild-Feather.

c r y i n g

Doris wanted him *inside* her.

Even though she was a virgin, she instinctively knew she wanted him inside her.

Her body possessed a programmable-memory-chip which opened an image of him-and-her unifying themselves together into *one*-body/*one*-love.

And although young Doris had never had an orgasm: her loneliness at times brought her to explore her clitoris.

Doris would sometimes gently-and-rhythmically rub it at night and felt the sensation rise-in-her.

However, after a couple of bouts with her hormones, young Doris decided that she wanted to wait for that climatic sensation...Doris wanted to wait for that special-*moment* with that special-someone.

Young Doris wanted to wait for a cherished-relationship of which she imagined with the aid of the *memory* of her parents' eyes when they looked into each other's eyes...that evident and visible strong love her parents shared for one-another.

Wild Feather gently raised her up from the sofa with both hands.

"Let's go get your dress!!!"

Both had purchased fabric last week for her dress. They then took it to a local tailor that Friday, May 31st 1968.

At the thought of all her ill mishaps leading to that day, Doris was beginning to give-in to her negativities.

However, it was Wild Feather's enthusiasm and positive-uplifting-spirits that brushed all those non-sense negative feelings aside from her insides.

The young woman Doris became excited!

[Excellent Doris!!! Good for you!:) J].

Doris kissed Wild Feather one-last-time before they began getting ready for the BIG-NIGHT!

[**hooray!**:)]

Young-Doris-was–all-smiles-and-so-was-he:)

[**Yippee! Great J!!!**:)]

 When they were ready, they jumped into his truck and sped off.

Doris had *completely* forgotten about *eV'REe-thing* that had happened in the hours preceding.

Doris had high hopes of dancing and **dancing**
and **dancing!**

[WOW! Yea J!]

There was to be an elaborative dinner prepared for
all of the high school seniors.

And the night was ONE-TO-REMEMBER.

[Yea!!!:)]

[Yup, those nights are usually filled with
Euphoria and great anticipation...being able to
participate with unlikely-classmates in a ritual of
fun brought a bundl*e*-load of fun-a***nd***-awkward
anticipation!]

awkward
anticipation!

[Oh wow! Do you remember your night!?]

[That's right, **you!:)**]

[yes I do J yes I do:) J]

The school had made arrangements with the city to occupy the city boardrooms and surrounding rooms to commemorate this special event: giving it an atmosphere of smallness but spaciousness at the same time.

Each room had something new and different to offer.

One room was devoted to jazz appreciation, another to classical music appreciation, another to rock and roll dancing, another to various ballroom dances, and another to desserts and main courses, and yet another to board games, and so on.

This was to be the most elegant and elaborate prom night the city had ever made! In the past they had made it small and simple: in the high school gym.

This year was special for several reasons. Some prominent sons and daughters of the city government were graduating that year, in addition to having a famous country singer's daughter graduating that year too!

Yes: influence of the affluent made *all the difference*; the resources and those able to command them were *at-hand* that year!

The night at-the-prom was beautiful and Doris had the TIME-OF-HER-LIFE! Wild Feather, for the first time, was dressed in a *black-and-white* t*ux*edo. [Yes folks! a TUX!:)]

Doris found him so attentive...So So So Attractive.

What pulled young Doris in was Wild Feather's enthusiasm to please her...going away from his *norm* to accommodate this *very-special-girl* on this night of her *PROM*.

At the **cease** of the festivities, everyone had *thoroughly* enjoyed themselves...including the Poindexters of the school!**:)** [oh my! I Hope and have Faith they didn't miss their New*to*nian club meeting!:)...it was by-the-way *scheduled* on that night!:)' HA HA HA...and The next night was Washing*ton* club night!.. ❯ ❯ ❯ Geek squad please *Exit* **To** Your ❮ ❮ *LEFT!* ❮ ❮ ❮ ❮ :)'...J!!:)''}

After this beautiful, well-coordinated celebration, as they drove home, Doris had her arms around Wild Feather. Doris leaned her head against his shoulders and never felt happier or safer.

This-was-the-*man*-of-her-dreams!

The man Doris wanted to live the rest of her life with: from the moment she became aware of him to the end of hers!

As Wild Feather parked the truck in front of the apartment and turned off the engine, he turned to Doris.

They embraced in a *warmth of love.*

warmth of love

He laid a kissed on her forehead while maintaining their embrace.

Wild Feather then went-out to-open-the-door for Doris.

As he carried her to the old apartment, Doris kept hugging him and kissing his neck.

Wild Feather returned the gesture with a kiss to her forehead.

That night was memorable since it was the night *Jana* came into being.

J a n a

As they entered, Wild Feather took her to his bedroom and gently laid her down on his twin-size bed.

As Doris lay gently on the sheets, Wild Feather delivered a passionate kiss to her lips.

...causing Doris to *electrify!*

The current of *conductivity* immediately became ignited into *two-nodes* contemplating a high energy flow!

An awakening into a realm of *perfect reciprocal oscillation* heading to a *central magnification.*

Doris wanted more!

Doris reached up to Wild Feather's ear and softly (but passionately-determined) said:

"I want you *in me*,"

"I want you more than anything **in** *this world.*"

Wild Feather stared at Doris for a moment.

He then kissed Doris and began to gently undress her.

He started with her dress, which was a bit of a challenge considering all the ornaments and underskirts.

They both laughed as he desperately tried to take it off.

Finally, after several attempts, Doris extended her arm and asked Wild Feather to help her to her feet.

As Doris stood there she turned around and directed Wild Feather (with her arms) to unzip the dress at particular locations.

It all then became easy after that.

After focusing on one arm at a time and then proceeding to another appropriate limb, Wild Feather finally was *able to free* **her** from her dress!

After taking the underskirts off as well, in a similar fashion, Wild Feather placed the garments on an old wooden chair by the door.

Doris waited for him.

Doris was now bare to her bra and lower underwear.

She looked marvelous with such soft gentle pink skin.

Wild Feather kissed every part of Doris from head to toe.

After his **commensal** but mutually beneficial savouring of her **commensuality!**, Doris proceeded with **gentleness-and-adroitness** to unbuckle Wild Feather's large cowboy belt...commencing to slowly undress him from his tuxedo garments.

When Doris finished, both stood there naked (with only their underwear on) embracing each other with **such** *warmth* that it looked (from a distance) as if they were *one body* in *perfect*

harmony with **itself**.

Wild Feather again gently laid Doris on the bed and began with an embrace of love that continued with a five minute kiss (that seemed to have *no ending)*.

no ending

As unwinding **Tension built:** the movements became more and more aggressive.

Aggressive!

The tension reached such a climax that both demanded the remaining garments to be **TORn off!**

OFF! TORN! TORN! OFF!

Doris reached for Wild Feather's underwear trying desperately to take them off, and Wild Feather proceeded with ripping hers off with one strong pull.

Doris wore (from top to bottom) specially tailored embroidered underwear (gently decorated with white flowery shapes).

Wild Feather began kissing her *bosom* uncontrollably.

He then began pressing up against her strongly.

Doris moaned and moaned and finally managed to rip Wild Feather's underwear right down the middle towards the back!

Doris quickly pulled them down and his penis was released!

released **PENIS***!*
PENIS released*!*

Doris stood up facing him and grabbed his PENIS and stroked it vigorously.

v i g o r o u s ly*!*

Doris kept the motion causing Wild Feather to moan and moan and forcing him to lift his head to the *sky*.

Wild Feather then moved closer to Doris and began directing his penis toward her.

...pushing and pushing up against her.

The penis began pushing against her vagina and the web around the Doris' vagina began to give way.

WEB WEB GIVE WAY WAY GIVE!

Doris was so wet inside that she no longer felt the pull but a rupture of pleasure as the penis *sought its home*.

HOME SAUGHT SAUGHT ITS HOME!

After a good 61 seconds of quick rhythmic pressing, Wild Feather was finally able to penetrate Doris' outer labias.

Doris burst out in a **SCREAM!**

She grabbed Wild Feather's thighs and pulled them towards her.

Wild Feather began rapid movements with his hips.....going further and further into Doris' vagina as her legs spread further and further apart.

FURTHER AND FURTHER APART!

Doris became more and more uncontrollable and **SCREAMED** uncontrollably!

Doris had never felt such **pleasure!**

PLEASURE FELT FELT PLEASURE!

Her love organ began going to autopilot and Doris began to **sweat** profusely.

fusely profusely SWEAT!

Doris' body kept on asking for more: she spread her legs as far apart as she could place them.

Doris then lifted them high above her head CAUSING her (by SO LIFTING) to feel his penis getting deeper-and-deeper inside her.

RUPTURE pleasure pleasure
R U P T U R E!

The movements began to get *completely out of control*! The bed began to squeak as if it were about to break!

BREAK BREAK BREAK!

Every time Wild Feather wanted to come COME COME COME! (but **H**e **H**ad **H**ad enough practice to keep the orgasm at a standstill: not giving it its desire of a climatic bliss).

The time however came when the hormones took dominance over his body: Wild Feather could hold it no longer and began to climax

to no return.

CLIMAX

NO RETURN

NO RETURN

CLIMAX

CLIMAX

CLIMAX

NO RETURN

Doris sensed it (having come several times...minutes before...during a *time* that was expanding as if its programming was being changed!).

as if its programming was being changed!

Wild Feather's increasing laud moans excited her to the point where Doris gave way to her

biggest *orgasm!*...

.. sending it off to the *Seas of Titan.*

S e a s of T i t a n

Doris came again with a **loud-long mooaan!**...triggering Wild Feather tc completely let go:

releasing the *splendor* of his sperms inside Doris!

After his initial **eruption**, Wild Feather kept pushing....... wanting to release every ounce of sperm *inside*-him-*into*-her.

inside-him-*into*-her

A gift perhaps?

.......to attempt to give all that you are to one that you love.

.......to give beyond what is human...an *energy flow*.

After a good two minutes after his ejaculation, Wild Feather began to go slower until finally he stationed his penis inside Doris.

Doris felt him inside and loved it!

She never wanted him to leave.

In return, Wild Feather felt such warmth of her that he did not want to leave either!!!...he wanted to be in her *safe haven* forever.

They both lay there in peace.

Both fell asleep.

After several lapses in time, Wild Feather was now slightly to his side and Doris remained wrapped in him.

After 52 minutes, both woke at the same time and looked at each other.

Both knew that this was a special moment that both had fought off for so long: but now consummated that longing.

CONSUMMATED
THAT *longing*.

Wild Feather kissed Doris on the lips and she immediately responded.

The lovemaking continued all-night-long; and into the afternoon the next day!

Neither wanted it to end.

Both were in wetness all around and adored the warmth that it brought.

Doris was by noon the next day completely full of sperm that she began dripping constantly.

Wild Feather lowered his head and began kissing Doris' vagina.

He then reached for Doris' hand and led her to the shower where both began cleansing each other.

Both were in a *state of paradise* and did not want it to end.

State of Paradise

...NOT WANT IT TO END.

Both took *every moment of time* and relished it as if it were SPECIAL FOOD to be consumed slowly:

paradise

state

time

m o m e n t

BLACKOUT

PART 5 of 7
JANA'S TRANSFORMATION

Chapter **20'3**
A Return to the PRE*SENT*
Jana Struggles To Write

Jana Stood there.

She stood there and she stood there.

Why was *she* writing?

What was *her* purpose?

WHO would benefit from it?

Jana contemplated these infringing thoughts that came into her mind.

Jana was caught in a *web* of self *eval*uation---- she questioned herself and she was not feeling good about it.

"Stop it Jana stop it!"

Jana yelled even louder at herself.

"STOP IT!"

Jana was beginning to feel emotional and the feelings intensified---She could not explain it.

But within the manipulations of her hormones and her memories-of-past, a pathway of *Demarka**TOR*** found its way!

Jana began to confront her negative self-analysis with peace instead of frustration and confusion.

Jana was beginning to understand the deceits of her body.

Any uneasiness was beginning to be consistently identified by her *Pensan-Transcend-Receptors* as THEMS (Tetra Hexanal Emissions Monstras SS-Cybers): the automotive hands of this *Matrix*.

Jana let the waters flow so that the currents had a clear pathway……. to a continuity of resistance!

Then Jana said to herself:

"Whatever the reason it is that I write I will *write*."

"For now my audience is me."

"My purpose is me."

"I write because it is what I have chosen to do."

"I write because I am compelled to tell a story for purposes that will become clear en tiempos ocultos."

"I will not judge myself"

"I WILL NOT!!!.....anymore."

"I will write in peace."

"I will tell what I must tell. ¡Compartir lo que se debe compartir!"

With that Sermon directed as a purpose to gain control of her encasement from the **demons**, Jana walked out of the room feeling strong.

Jana had commanded peace while placing a positive outlook on her activity to *write*.

Jana grabbed her things and headed to the boardwalk to refresh her commitment to herself: ...to give *air* back its *elements*...retaining only what is of true nature before the *contamination*.

BEFORE THE *CONTAMINATION*

As Jana entered the beach boardwalk, people there were walking and admiring large luxurious homes owned by other human beings.

Some had **nip-pits** of envy pierce their programming...creating a wedge of TRIANGULAR MODULATION that consisted of: jealousy, admiration, and anger.

admiration, anger, jealousy

...Ingredients **precisely** ENGINEERED for the purpose of:

> weakening and transforming the spirit (eternal energy) by...

> ...fortifying implants that would yield decades of distraction with the ultimate goal of having these implants permanently embedded even after the death of the encasement.

...an **attachment** that would transcend states of being: creating a ready-for-consumption <u>energy-pack</u> (*resistance*-free) for 𝕽**a**!

𝕽**a**!

𝕽**a**!

Chapter Twenty Four

Standing Bow
(Jana's Character Evolves)

As Jana walked on the boardwalk she felt an inner peace.

Everything was moving well for her.

She had nothing to complain about; not even her inner workings (since those were works in progress and being resolved a moment at a time).

Jana had no school lesson-plans to write, no rent to pay, no food to pay---Miguel insisted on paying all the expenses including Jana's Euclid apartment rent.

Jana had insisted on *retaining* her own personal place.

In her mind, Jana felt she still needed a place to feel some sort of independence---although it was becoming clear that what was happening was the complete *opposite*!

Miguel loved her and she knew it.

Jana loved him even *more!*

Jana truly felt wanted, needed, loved, appreciated!

Jana felt secure with Miguel, and his passionate love making made her feel so-so-so good.

Jana would come at least **seven-times** every time they were together. Sometimes as much as 16: little pleasurable **Sambhōga-ru Kogarana** at every point of her sex organ...from every tip of her inner vagina to the outer labias to her clitoris.

小柄なオルガスムの喜び

嬌小高潮的喜悅

□□□ □□ □□□□ □□□

And once they had experimented with anal sex. At first it was unpleasant for Jana; but then she found arousal in this bonding by her ***pure desire*** to have him *everywhere* he could possibly be...***physically***.

The thought of this "everywhere" excited Jana that she would come even if her clitoris was not touched...emotions rang high!

Now that Jana was pregnant, Miguel was soft yet forceful at the moments of her orgasms.

The array of **chemicals** at orgasm (including **oxytocin, prolactin,** and **endorphins**) that were produced and poured-out -into her body came plentiful and a huge relaxation always left Jana exhausted and sleepy----it appears more so now than before she b*eka-Me* pregnant.

Besides the great sex, Miguel often talked about how beautiful it would be to have a ceremony as an expression of their love.

Jana wanted such a public expression but refused to add the legality to it.

To Jana: making it "legal" really made no difference in the 'love' she held deeply for Miguel.

For Jana, such an intrusive action as putting the government between their love just made no sense.

Jana was well aware of the high divorce rate and all the improprieties that such a legal action entailed and wanted no part in it!

Legal Marriage spelled Ugliness for Jana.

Jana wanted to maintain a *taint-free* love.

Deep inside the *eternal mind* of Jana...her *offerings* of love came as-pure-as she knew the meaning of the *true word* from which the word "love" perpetrated to synonymize.

As Jana walked north on the boardwalk she decided to take the bridge overpass to *Ocean*[*us*] Avenue.

Jana walked briskly since she wanted to maintain some sort of workout during her *pregnancy*.

Jana headed toward the Barnes and Noble on *Wil*shire and *Third* Street.

She wanted to glance on the culture of the boy she was writing about. Jana looked at several books and read several captions and paragraphs—but did not want to go deep into research just yet.

Jana wanted to be able to free-write first and fill-in-the-details later—giving CREATIVITY a solo venue to *exercise* its *Wings* away from turbulences (avoiding any sabotaging programmable e-eddies or minions-of-the-*light*).

Some inspiration away from the stupidities of life.

Unconsciously Jana was reaching for *pathways* in her Native American genes that moved within her...a connection activity Jana still hadn't consciously made into an ongoing exercise.

Her ultra-mind was seeking to somehow close the gaps-and-turns that twisted her eternal being: metaphysically aligning the divisions within her energy by undoing her genes to **before** their intrusions...the created makeup.

Consciously, Jana wanted to be genuine to those inherent parts within her (both Native American and Irish genes) that live and vibrate within her.

Although those *vibrations* were hidden from her because of the human veil placed on her, Jana was determined to be ONE-with-herself and *solidify* the *eternal connection.*

WINDOWS, she felt, deeply resided in her.

And from these WINDOWS, Jana was determined to write the stories that sought *manifestations* for reasons unknown to her.

Jana spent about two hours there looking over pages of material that *provoked* **inh**er an urge to write.

After her analysis session at the bookstore, Jana hurried *home.*

As Jana walked briskly back toward the bridge over pass, she tripped and went flying--- everything seemed to be moving in slow motion, or maybe she took control of time!

Control of time!

With the slow pacing she was *experienc*ing in time, Jana was able to think and react in the best *way* possible.

Jana tilted herself to the left and brought her legs forward, allowing her to land on her feet---the floor screeched but she was not injured.

Jana was amazed at her reflex, how everything slowed for her, and how she was able to avoid injury to herself and the child she had within her.

Jana paused and looked up into the *cloudless* sky.

Jana took the opportunity to center her *energy*.

…to make an introduction of sorts to an unknown in her bodily *consciousness*.

Jana attempted to mend the currents.

Jana was not sure of anything or how it works but felt that the mend was underway!

underway!
mend mend mend

Jana smiled from cheek bone to check bone...and the boundless-smile-within-her-was-even-*greater*!

The **TRANSCENDENTAL** journey was definitely
DEFIANTLY {away from Ra} *underway*!

Jana knew it.

And the process manifesting itself within Jana is
Faith **and in serene peace** where Hope is already
attained!

Jana began her *pace* and continued toward
home---the home toward her eternal mind and to
her writing and to her destiny.

Upon arrival to her home, Jana felt hungry... but
refused to give the body food until she wrote some
more.

Jana began to write:

Standing Bow stood by the stream where

his tribe's settlement positioned themselves

during that hot season in August.

He placed his feet in the stream and felt the

cold water rushing around them...it felt

refreshing.

Soon the cold water ran over to all of his body causing his overall temperature to drop.

At first his muscles stiffened and then relaxed. The refreshment continued.

The refreshment however did not reach his thoughts. Standing Bow deeply grieved for his parents who showed signs of despair on their faces because of the lost of their eldest son who they could neither claim dead nor alive.

As the years past, Standing Bow became a fierce warrior at the age of seventeen.

He had perfected his skills both on foot and

on horse.

Whenever he found himself in battle, either with the white man or a warring tribe, he completely became a killing tool.

His parents and the rest of his tribe resisted being swept by the white man (or any collaborator for the white man).

His tribe was peculiar in that they preferred to be on foot in battle as much as they enjoyed it on horse.

And although they had access to firearms, pillaged from the white man and other tribes, they preferred their own weapons that had been passed on from generation to generation.

The bow and arrow represented a trade and a skill not easily acquired.

The bow and arrow were unique instruments which were made from tree wood of cherry, ash, willow, hickory, juniper, oak, Osage orange, cedar, walnut and birch trees.

But Standing Bow's tribes almost exclusively used the wood from the Osage orange tree because of its abundance.

The wood was uniquely strong yet flexible: allowing the construction of the bow to be longer than most other tribe's bows, providing a stronger thrust for accuracy...making the precision "standard" highly desirable.

Standing Bow's tribe made the bow's string from sinew, animal entrails, hide, or plant fibers (whatever was readily available depending on the season and other factors).

The arrowhead was made from sharpened stone or flint, but sometimes also from metal obtained from the white man.

The arrow was about half the size of the bow from dried wood. The end tip of the arrow was made of feather obtained from eagles, hawks, turkeys, or any other available bird.

The feather provided an indispensable element to the arrow which balanced the weight of the arrowhead while creating a spinning effect making its trajectory to its target extremely accurate.

With the warring skills acquired from years of practice beginning at early childhood, Standing Bow and the other warriors became efficient predators and protectors...being able to circumvent the fastness of the white man's fire-weapons...keeping safe their tribe.

The horse (an efficient animal introduced by the Spanish white-man) brought them out of the Shoshone establishment and made them into a unique warrior tribe to be feared by any other tribe or encroacher.

This group of Native Americans became known as "The Comanche" by those who feared them.

Standing bow did not like to kill but it was not a choice decision (but rather a matter of kill or be killed).

Leaving any enemies alive would create a danger of having them return in greater numbers.

This Comanche tribe would bury their enemies and give them the same burial rites they themselves received when they lost one of their own; one of their loved ones.

Standing Bow had many options to settle down with one of the available young girls of the tribe. But, he refused them all. He knew the pain of losing many good friends, comrades, in battle. And he did not want to give grief to a maiden in the event that he perished during battle.

His parents encouraged him to seek the comforts of a woman, but Standing Bow refused even them this wish for his son. This was completely awkward since the other warriors did not share his view.

However, there was this one maiden who made every gesture to attract him to her.

Her name was Tlatletla.

Ttlatletla was persistent and decided to keep herself pure in hopes that one day she could marry and love Standing Bow.

Years past and she refused to give in to other warriors. Her parents called her crazy because she had refused so many fine

> looking warriors.
>
> Her parents consistently counseled her to forget Standing Bow.
>
> Ttlatletla would not give up.
>
> Ttlatletla's hopes were high despite the present odds.

Jana thought, "Wow, what a woman!"

The new writer continued to evolve her story:

> On his twentieth day on this Earth, Standing Bow found himself surrounded by a group of white men and enemy natives who had agreed to work with the white man together to snuff out or neutralize Standing Bow's tribe.

The battle began at day break while Standing Bow and his men were patrolling on horse their area five miles East of where his family and that of all his people were settled.

Standing Bow's mission was to protect the tribe and repel any encroachments by the enemies.

As it turned out, they were outnumbered five to one.

The plains were open and they headed on their horses to a slope of rocks for protection against the gun fire coming at them.

But before reaching safety, many warriors fell as they attempted to dodge the bullets coming from the direction they were heading toward!

One side of the battlefield seemed to have the least amount of enemy combatants and it was there that the mountainous slopes were.

The tribe's warriors' quick maneuvers also killed many enemies with the spear and with the bow and arrow.

From the direction that they were heading, the remaining six white men soldiers and three enemy natives near the rocks who did not fall were at the center still blocking their way.

The other enemies began closing in on them from all directions.

It was a necessity to make this passage to the rocks available now!

Standing Bow yelled out to his comrades in the Comanche language, "make left, make left and shoot triples!"

The men responded quickly and made left and grasped 3 arrows and stretched them out in their bow as far back as possible while riding on their horses.

Standing Bow did likewise but in the direction of right. He praised the gods, yelled at his men, and they released their arrows.

All arrows flew with complete accuracy from the years of practice straight into their victims' upper torsos.

This disabled the human wall in front of them and the rest of the warriors were able to pass.

As Standing Bow passed he felt a burning sting on his tired right shoulder.

He turned right with his bow ready and aimed it at the culprit who had caused him the burn.

He released the arrow straight into his enemy's left eye; more arrows followed from his comrades passing by.

The enemy fell dying.

Jana stood up and visualized the battle scene.

"The struggles they faced are struggles that are continual"---she thought. "Always outnumbered but never giving up!"

Jana paced around the living room in warrior movement and stance.

Somehow she knew how to do it (not needing to think about it). The *flow of energy* from within her guided her every step…her every stance.

After much movement, Jana sat back down to her lap-top and wrote what she had thought last,

Always outnumbered...

but never giving up!

Jana stared for quite a while at the words she had just written:

Always outnumbered …

But never giving up!

"My struggles aren't those right now", she thought.

Jana was grateful with everything in her present---
-everything except her past.

Jana wanted to see her mother and her father.

Jana knew where her mother was but not her
father.

Jana was now about over 2 months along and
signs of her pregnancy were beginning to show.
She would soon need to buy clothing that would
fit her changing body size to allow the natural
growth of the baby and its womb.

Despite her good present and her hopes for mom
and dad, Jana still was not complete in many ways
in her mind:

…the change within Jana's mind had not yet
unfurled completely.

…it sought a solid connection to her *eternal self!*

Jana's relationship with her mother was a distant
one: Jana LONGED-to-*bind*-it-closer.

.....and she wanted so so so much much to see father.

Jana GRIEVED his absence.

"Where is daddy!??",

is what Jana would utter in her mind many many many times at points in her life up-to-the-present; and many times the *extract*ion caused loneliness and tears. ',','','','','','' , '' , , '' ,''

These were the hang ups that were *deep inside* Jana. These kept her `static` many times.

Jana would convince herself that they were not hang ups.

But NOW were NOT the pasts.

NOW NOT PASTS

PASTS NOT NOW!

The time had come to face the truth and not pretend anymore.

These hang-ups were not the only piece that needed working!

In order to provide lasting ***peace*** within herself, Jana needed to mend ties and come to really know who she was and were she *truly* came from.

Jana knew that to some extent…somewhere *in-a-consciousness*.

And so subconsciously Jana began to write in order to clarify the energies within herself—PEELING-THE-CARBON that hid those energies that tied her to her ancestors and ultimately to her eternity!

The LIQUID FORM of her encased energy rendered her weak, especially in her initial attempts to find the truth.

It was as though her eternal self was neutralized: the liquefied form seemed to allow the manipulation of her energy to begin a planned-intent energy transformation she resisted!

JANA RESISTED!

Most humans are unaware of this plan!

…being distracted by the gatekeepers and the necessities to survive a perceived temporal world.

[and so should you resist! yes you... my lovely reader. **Resist!**]

Chapter 25 [7]
JaMiWeVaPe
(Shesha Returns)

When Miguel arrived that evening, Jana greeted him with a kiss at the door and pressed herself against him---Jana could feel the rush of hormones wanting him right-then-and-there.

Miguel was caught by surprise.....but it was a pleasant surprise.

Miguel reciprocated a similar gesture.

They made love from those seconds to minutes to hours.

At one point Jana stroked Miguel's penis with her hands and then at another point she lowered herself to meet it face to face.

Jana opened her mouth and took him in: rhythmically moving her head back and forth as Miguel began to moan.

As Jana intensified her pace Miguel began to yell and involuntarily grabbed her hair and forced more of himself into her mouth.

Jana had grown very fond of Miguel's hard, thick, dark penis.

In one gigantic gasp, after about seven minutes, Miguel spurt out his semen into Jana's mouth.

Jana received his semen with pleasure: and let it drip out of her mouth and onto her chest.

Miguel began to *buckle* at the knees.

All the while, Jana spread the semen all over her body, as if it were cream, which after a while dried up on her.

Miguel stood from his *spent* position and then lifted Jana up. They embraced. One *spent* and the other wanting to be *spent*!

Jana led him to the bedroom, undressed him and laid him on the bed. She then spread her thighs apart and sat on top of his penis...it was soft yet pleasurable to feel with her outer vagina...her **LABIAS**.

Slowly but consistently Jana began to stroke Miguel's penis with her **mo i s t LABIAS**, bringing it to *life* once more!

Miguel's penis (whom she affectionately referred to as **Don Quixote**) began to rise and stiffen!

The **Don** wanted to revive the Chivalry of Romance... again!!!!!!!

Jana curled down and spoke to it. "Oh, look at you. You look ready for battle!"

"Let me kiss you and hug you Mr. Quixote!"

Jana began kissing it and hugging it with her mouth.

The intensity **INTENSIFIED!**

ELECTR/FIED!

As **Don Quixote** stiffened to her liking, Jana went on top of it again, and with her *left* hand, guided the penis into her.

Don Quixote PENETRATED the Vagina and Jana began to moan.

Jana moaned...and

... and moaned...and moaned!

As Jana raised and lowered herself on top of Mr. Quixote, her moans became longer and LOUDER!

Miguel laid there delightfully watching Jana as she rose and descended in pleasure.

pleasure!

placer

plezi   Furaha

愉楽(Yuraku)

HAZ Задоволення

(Zadovolennya)

Miguel had come earlier, enabling him to resist any temptation of wanting to come tuuoo early to interrupt Jana's MANIFESTING-EXCITEMENT!

Ðon Quixote became her

TOTEM
POLE
OF
PLEASURE.

As the **RHYTHM** increased its pace, Jana grasped Miguel's hands and directed them to her ass where he grasped them firmly and began pulling them down to himself.

Jana felt the forcefulness and began to moan even louder as she increased her pace.

The feeling was unbearable and Jana began to yell loudly as if in pain, as if someone was hurting her.

Miguel became startled but continued.

As the rhythm *condensed* into *one-long-note*: Jana came in a SEA OF WETNESS that made flapping sounds.

Jana cried out "Ahhhhhhhhhh!!!" ...*expelling* every-bit-of-air from her lungs.

The pace slowed and Jana was completely untwined at her seams.....moving toward complete-exhaustion.

Jana placed her body down and laid on top of Miguel, **BREATHING** deeply in loud silence.

Miguel received Jana and embraced her while still having his hard-penis inside-her.

After a while, Miguel laid her down on his bed while keeping himself inside her.

.....Some sort of an artistic acrobatic move!

It was a beautiful display of skill!

Miguel then said, "my turn" and with that he raised her legs to his shoulders and began pouncing on Jana.

Jana began to moan and recover as Miguel forcefully penetrated her as-never-before.

After a good 10 minutes, Miguel increased his pace: which prompted Jana to voice: "I'm coming aaaa**A**ah**G**ai**N**, please **DON'T** stop!"

Miguel continued: further increasing his speed.

As Miguel came: letting out his last bit of semen: Jana burst into a moan of **ORGAZMOS** and CAME **ONCE MORE***!*

This was **a session** MORE OF LUST THAN OF LOVE.

It was definitely LUST **OVER** LOVE.

The hormones had gotten their way.

The couple laid there:

....**BOTH** completely **S**pent.

Both **FULL OF semen**.

Both full of an abundance of **vaginal secretions**.

Both *covered* in **ecstasy** from the *inside- out!*

out!   *out!*   *Out!*

Both Love Birds (rather Lust Birds) slept slept
slept

Neither one aware of the other's presence.

Both in their separate dreams.

Both in their separate rests.

At about three in the morning, naked Jana awoke
and noticed Miguel flat on the bed---his
luscious dark skin revealing his muscular thighs,
back, buttocks, and arms caused her hormonal
sensations from within.

What a complete attractive specimen of a human male.

"My man, my love, my lover", thought Jana as she BREATHED-IN the sight!

After a mesmerizing intake, Jana stood and headed into the bathroom to clean herself up.

Semen was still coming out of her vagina and the dry semen caked-like-thick-frosting remained all-over-her-body (¡incluso su cara!).

Jana raised her arms in front of her and, with her hands, she massaged her body circularly: feeling the roughness of the outer dry semen.

creating the prison...

Semen. Spermatozoa. Spermatozoon. Ovum.

Egg

Fuse

GlycoProteins

Reaction

Division

Replication

Mitosis

Chromosomes

Mitotic Spindle

E n c a s e m e n t Complete!

Jana then felt the wetness of her vagina…

—**smooth** and soft.

Jana then caressed her skin above her womb.

Her pregnancy still was not exaggeratedly noticeable as having a child within: but Jana knew he or she was there.

Jana went to the left-large-circular mirror which was between the first two sinks (each of which had a diamond shape mirror in front of it) and stared at the reflection in front of her:

A woman full of **pain** and full of **joy!**

...A **paradox** that could only be **human.**

h   u   m   a   n

Jana smiled at herself and said "hi" as if introducing herself to herself.

"How are you doing? How are you feeling?" Jana said with a somewhat *slithering-of-words* into *one-long-strand*: fluxuating the volume with her entire respiratory system in a sine-cosine curve...as if having trouble breathing...ASTHMATIC like.

There stood Jana in front of *thAt* image.

Jana stared at herself trying to look deeper; trying to understand who she really was WITHOUT *thAt* genetic make-up... *thAt* image in the mirror.

A **Snap-shot** of *light* then **Entered** Jana.

Jana thought of her dad and of her mom.

Jana thought of her **G**reat-**G**rand-**P**arents and all her ancestors she never knew.

Jana thought of the hundreds of thousands of ancestral years of people who are part of her **G**enetic **B**eing: those she had not had the opportunity to know personally or consciously in mind.

```
        c o n s c i o u s l y
        i n   m i n d . . . .
```
V   o I ded...

The human mind.

.....Those ancestors that at times Jana felt inside but NOT BEING ABLE TO fully-

G R A S P the images of their *aura* (a barrier CAUSED BY a ***cloudness of film*** produced by the CARBON encasement which distracted her from knowing-them-fully).

As Jana stared at herself she spoke to them in thought: " I will see you when I *die*.".

At that conclusion, Jana snapped out of her trance and proceeded to the shower.

Jana rinsed herself renewing her body to where it *once came*.

The liquid energy poured over Jana at first cold then leveled off warm.

Jana passed her hands over her entire body with a *pink* sponge filled with SABUN and SU.

After creating a *white* lather Jana softly covered her body with it. Once the body was fully engulfed with ***it*** (W), she rinsed ***it*** (B).....renewing ***it*** (B).

IT.

After taking a deep breath, Jana stepped out of the shower and lightly dried herself.

Jana began feeling sleepy and decided to submit-herself-to-her-unconsciousness.

Jana did not want to wake Miguel, so after whispering *"I love you"* to him as she passed him, she proceeded to the living room couch.

Jana lay down and sl*ept* sl*ept* sl*ept*!

Quickly Jana began to dream and felt quite comfortable in that **un**conscious **state**.

Although aware in the beginning of her dream-state...Jana soon fell deeper into this *frame of reference*...losing consciousness of where she was.

Jana's dream-state images at first were just black images with no coherent storyline. It was a state of consciousness where she still could operate *reflective thought.*

Soon however when she truly-entered-into-the-unconsciousness-of-her-mind, Jana felt an image of *wind* brush her face.

She felt it as if it were *real!*

[What is *real* but a perceived interpretation of `programmed-electrical-signals!`]

[`Signals` created by an *author* for a particular purpose!]

[What is this *Pur-Pose*?]

 S*oon* Jana began entering a world that she could not figure out because of the *psyche* created by her environmental-programmed-mind:

… *W*here the dream-world and the *perpetrated* wake-world are not given equal-validity in terms of perceived-"true"-*real*ities*!*

Many times dreams are categorized as not-being-"*real*".

But this *wind* was "*real*" and Jana began seeing a dirt path on which she was walking.

Jana looked up at the night sky which was dark but warm.

Stars filled its emptiness!

Jana could smell the prairie dirt as it *rose* to her senses.

Familiarity began to materialize in her mind *onto* an unfamiliar place.

Jana instinct*ly* lowered herself to the ground and began making movements in a squatted position that seemed normal but where in fact actions she had not taken in the *wake*-world.

Jana then lowered her *hand*s onto the ground...a ground that felt wet-but-warm.

Jana then lowered her whole body, including her face, down onto the ground: taking in further the earth smell to her senses: providing her A STRENGTH within that *witch* she had never felt before.

Jana felt THE STRENGTH going into her being and energizing it.

Jana placed her *left* ear directly to the ground and began to hear rumbling.

Jana was *looking* with her ear for movement of the buffalo she was pursuing.

As Jana distinctly heard the buffalo sound, she knew it was coming from the *east*.

Suddenly Jana heard footsteps approaching, she did not turn around.

A *voice* yelled, "Shesha".

The well formed Native American woman spoke to the *voice* in Comanche, "Father, they are four leagues east and running. Bring forth my horse: let's capture them while darkness still ascends".

Jana was now Shesha and acted as if she had always been Shesha.

In this world Jana realized subconsciously consciously (for the first time) who she was, once *in-a-time*. Although, in her "wake" state, this knowledge was clouded by the filter (the human brain).

Shesha's father brought the horse and Shesha without looking back turned her body left guided by the sound of the approaching horse and leapt on it with precision!

As Shesha landed, she pulled out her bow and arrow from the pouch located to the right side of the horse's mane.

Before she roared in a gallop, Shesha yelled at the tribe's warriors who were behind her, "Slatla, Fatcha, Bonchela break left and stelthfully go now!"

"Sitcha, Platza, Micza break right, go now!"

"Santle, Ecklentla, Cklalala stay behind and follow now!"

Jana and her father's tribe's warriors followed suit quickly but stealthfully.

Her father stayed at the tail to supervise the operation.

After about three leagues, Jana could smell the Buffalo: she began *craving* the meat she pictured in her mind and began getting into a frenzy.

KRÄVA

Her limbs began violently waving side to side and Shesha gave her horse three kicks, commanding it to swiftly increase its speed.

Shesha's head began to bob from left to right, and from diagonal to diagonal.

This became more and more *intense* as she approached the buffalo.

As the *end-points* began **shrinking** the distinal space between them, the buffalo began running more as the beasts visually spotted the intruders.

Shesha took the first shot at a buffalo of seven and stifled its movement by landing the arrow behind its massive neck; the others in her group shot their arrows at the beast and slowed it down considerably: allowing the jumper to leap on the beast and begin to stab it repeatedly with a knife.

The beast began to limp. And, after several **everlasting** moments of struggle resisting wholeheartedly, the best violently fell to its side and began breathing its last breathes*!*

The other two groups did likewise to their chosen buffalo.

Each group successfully conquered its prey.

Each group was assigned only one-full-grown-buffalo.

On that preyful-*dawn*ish-night, their targets consisted of *seven* full-grown beasts and *four* small cubs.

PREYافتراس

PRESA شکار

PRESA শিকার

獵物

Victory was sweet.

IMPANGO

in-^ya-^thi

Each member of each group knew his or her job that came after the catch.

The duties consisted of skinning the beast, cutting the meat, preparing storage of the various goods the buffalo provided: everything from the hide for coat manufacturing, beef jerky, tools from the bones and hairs, and so on.

More intrinsic duties were performed by other non-warrior members such as the women, children, and the elderly of the tribe.

Not one item of the beast was left behind, except for the excess BLOOD that flowed *to the ground* as they did their procedural work after the kill.

Any excess blood that did not sink underneath the ground was buried.

They *left* NOT-A-TRACE of the conquest!

Only the keen olfactory organs of the *W*ild could sense what went on in THAT area of the prairie.

No Blood Was Seen

Only

Horizon

Horizon

beyond the

Horizon

Shesha then found herself alone in darkness.

She could not veer which way was home.

VEER WHICH WAY WAS HOME

Suddenly *a-point-in-time* came where complete SILENCE crept in:

Shesha could not hear a sound *nor* could she feel the wind blow anymore.

It was as though "*the programming*" had changed right beneath her feet!

Shesha squatted and sat down with her legs crossed.

She placed her hands on her knees and *closed* her eyes.

Shesha sat in *perfect harmony* with her bones and with her muscles and with her blood....aligning her complete body in such a way that she became *completely-at-rest*.

Shesha came-into-a-trance and felt her body stay behind as she SOARED toward the sky.

Shesha was no longer breathing.

Shesha was no longer smelling or hearing or sensing.

Shesha was *a spirit* (an eternal energy) on-a-mission.

mission

Her mission was to hold guard over the ENERGIES within the human bodies as they SLEPT....both the living, and those near their dead human bodies...those still trapped in this world in this planet in this Universe not knowing their true nature...confused...those that believed the lie:

Ghosts!

Shesha had transformed into Pure Energy...a servant of the *Intrinsic-God* (a part of God as all energies are) that allowed her to exist **out-of-its-***ekhaya realm* (the point of origin up to where the rebellion begins...where the violent-unsteady-unsound-fiery flamed-deceitful various UNIVERSES GROUNDS exist!).

YONKE UMHLABATHI

Also known as the

THE SLEEP REALMS

Shesha was **NOT A BELIEVER** of multiple gods but rather of ONE GOD over all other beings.

One creator of all that is, was, and will always be.

Shesha knew GOD as ONE BODY WITH ITS MANY PARTS.

A Virus Had infected the ONE BODY...allowing PARTS OF IT to be pushed out!...with it went other CELLS.

A group of those CELLS are the ones assigned to Shesha.

CELLS imprisoned in this realm [where you and I live.], and other distant realms [where brothers and sisters live!]

As Shesha reached the **outer~areas** of the Earth's atmosphere, her energy dispersed itself outwards over the Earth, and other assigned areas of the universes, into an oval-shape direction (doing all this while co-existing in the Realm **BEFORE** Creation of the Universes...from which she gathered her **STRENGTH** to combat the demons...agents of **Ra**!).

Shesha began to **sway** back and forth from one ends-of-the-Earth to the other with her AXIS **securely-set**.

The **movements** vibrated on all-points-of-time; making "speed" irrelevant!

The ENERGY was at work...gathering other strands into its path....making **Ra**'s objectives non-sense as Shesha imprinted her presence in all of **TIMES'** set *motions*...bringing parts of the universes to a close.

All rejuvenations to Origin are a product of Jesus.

Jesus…the Only Path that leads to **Home.**

Her partners, the other ENERGIES also assigned the dismantling of the Creations, around the other rebelled areas, began closing their assigned spots and shrinking the universes and placing its motions to a still.....**E**ncompassing its space and absorbing it through the **REFINEMENT** PATH-WAY before joining the ONE BODY.

These ENERGIES OF GOD are specifically protecting against the agents of **Ra** and the other **rebellious STARS**...a constant battle while the Universes are allowed to exist!

Manifesting THEMSELVES against particular stations in **TIMES**.

Shesha the human did not know completely the **hidden** but her ETERNAL ENERGY did know.

This ENERGY knew what it was commanded to do and what companion ENERGIES to use as it swayed over the Earth, and other parts of the Universes. [Yes, WE work in groups!]

Shesha accepted her programmed being serving the bigger purpose. She was content because its circuits were coming into fruitful fruitions.

 Shesha saw the **glimpse** of a **TIME** to come (and a **TIME** passed). Her present station in the **PROGRAMMED ELEMENT** is also known as **TIME**.

Shesha knew also that the G R I D of complete collapse of the universe and universes…(where the rebellion would be permanently snuffed out completely)…had **not yet** been assigned.

Everything serves a purpose.

Everything has a fate.

Everything comes together at an appointed G R I D.

Nothing is by chance.

[which is in contrast, **U**nlike, to those inaccuracies committed by **Ra** and the other **Stars**…where they seek to be exact but fail at their attempts…and to **extract** ALL but fail there as well.]

[For there is **no other power** greater than that of **THE SOURCE**…from which all originate…our home and our rest…where Father God lives!: ¡Aleluya!]

The ONE BODY could never be overruled for it serves ALL, because it is ALL.

The manifested "𝕽𝖊𝖇𝖊𝖑𝖑𝖎𝖔𝖓" was allowed to be set in motion to fulfill REALIZATIONS within the ONE BODY.

As *dawn* arrived, Shesha returned to her body and became one with it.

Suddenly all around her she felt A BREEZE and it swept her into a whiteness.

Shesha opened her eyes and woke-as-Jana!

In coming into this new consciousness within a consciousness, Jana took a deep-inhalation-of-*shock*!

"What was that!?" She asked.

Jana could now remember her dream and did not forget what had transpired in this reality labeled a dream.

Jana was *privied* a window to the past and to the future!...to the *grids*

GRIDS

Jana was becoming more and more in tune with this reality; and her connection to her other self

was **beginning** to mesh into *one*.

Jana now considered her identity as also being that of *Shesha*.

Jana PAUSED her thought for some time

PAUSED

...Feeling her **synapses** quickly **running** the **images** she had **witnessed**: reminding herself in her mind so that she would not forget.

Everything became so vivid in her mind. A *nestle* hole was prepared for this memory. Jana made sure it was well categorized so as to reference it when needed.

Jana sat up in the couch, placed her feet on the ground, took a deep breath:

a spark of thought **entered her mind.**

ENTERED HER MIND *a spark* of thought entered and she said:

"I must go…

I must go…

I must go to...

I must go to... ... ..."

a *moment's* PAUSE **AMPLIFIED** *the spark:*

"O K L A H O M A !".

Chapter **Twenty 6**
Oklahoma

Jana wanted to return to her home state of Oklahoma (her birth place) to find answers to attempt to resolve unresolved issues in her past...and to understand better the dreams she had been encountering up to the present.

Past issues consisted of Jana wanting to make **amends** with her **mother** (somehow **find a way** to get closer to her), **find her father**, and to resolve other delicate matters that **still** haunted her.

In the past Jana had sought help through psychologists as to her rape in college by *that* massive jock woman, finding avenues to resolve disappointments in her past intimate relationships, and more.

None of the three psychologists that she went to were able to *place-peace*-in-Jana's *m*ind.

The Psychologists were unable to find those missing-pieces of the puzzle to resolve her bouts of amnesia, insomnia, faintness, sudden angers, and an array of other psychological symptoms that many times manifested themselves into physical symptoms.

Besides these so-called-doctors, Jana did not share her issues with anyone.

In her mind, Jana consciously sought to contain her issues from affecting other people.

Jana was very conscientious of others and wanted to always treat others better than herself: even though there came `points-in-time` were she almost lost her cool with others as she often did with herself.

Maybe Jana needed to lose her cool with certain individuals in order to understand herself better or to make better judgments of people?...not ignoring apparent red-flags or moving in naïvetés.

naïvetés

[We all are vulnerable to that in the beginning...some continue!]

Not sustaining though, at this stage in her life, Jana's **bouts**-in-time with herself were becoming **less** and **less** frequent.

Jana was evolving into not being so critical with herself...appreciating MORE-and-MORE the discovery of who she is, and what she is to truly be.

truly be

There *stood* Jana.

...on a platform ready to take flight...not with her own wings yet!...but with those provided by Boeing.

Jana was at the airport.

It was the 17th of November 2007.

An announcement came on the P.A., "Now boarding flight 340...". It was 7 in the morning and Jana had decided that she needed to be in Muskogee, Oklahoma early....the place she ultimately grew up at when her mother moved to a smaller city within the state.

The closest domestic airport to Muskogee was in Tulsa, Oklahoma.

Jana's plan was to rent a car to drive to Muskogee from the airport....an approximate 52 mile car trip.

After collecting her small navy blue duffle bag, Jana proceeded with *anticipation* to the door of the aircraft.

People were around her but Jana was **too focused** on what she may or may not *do* once in Oklahoma.

At that very moment Jana was more contemplative than social.

Miguel was very supportive of Jana going to her home-state. He knew she needed to sort out issues from her past: delicate items Jana spoke little about to him or anyone.

Jana had a *time-bomb* that needed to be diffused.

That

B O M B

kept her on the edge.

Miguel wanted to help facilitate the dismantling of that ***bomb-bomb-bomb*** he knew little about.

In his mind it was imperative that Jana find the peace she sought. Miguel could see and feel the struggle to attain peace in her eyes.

The empathy between the couple was growing: it was as though they were becoming *twins* in many ways. [a remarkable thing in a relationship!]

Habits between them began moving like *A*lternating-*C*urrents envisioned in the eyes-of-*Tesla*!

Jana felt the *new*-being inside her. It was patient it was kind she thought, "putting up with all my insecurities".

At about over 2 months into her pregnancy, the *being* within her was humanly maturing.

Jana did not yet buy any maternity clothing for herself but did make adjustments to her pants as to the waist, slightly opening them about an inch wider...sustaining them with her belt.

Jana's dresses and skirts still fitted her well; and since summer was coming-to-being, she would wear more dresses and skirts than pants.

In the past Jana would rarely wear underwear. She felt more ventilated without them, and the action of keeping them off made her feel freer.

But now, with the new *being* in her, Jana felt she should wear them as some sort of cover-for-its-home.

Miguel had purchased Jana her first-class ticket to Oklahoma. She felt special. Jana always in the past flew by coach.

As Jana entered the plane and was directed to her seat, she immediately felt **special** in seeing the wide space and accommodations being presented to her.

"Thank you Miguel!" Jana whispered under her breathe with a smile.

The flight went well and Jana did not put much thought on anything while in *flight*.

The *lift off* was smooth.

And once **airborne**, Jana reclined her seat and took deep breaths; intentionally not thinking much and just resting and staring at the ceiling of the plane: making numerous images formed by the crevices (and playing with them).

Her imagination at times went *rampant*!

Jana dare not fall asleep because she knew she may dream and thus *think*.

Jana was relaxed and happy she was taking-the-*trip*.

In her past, when Jana first departed Oklahoma to California, her mother had grown even more cold towards her: rarely taking the time to call her back when she phoned.

Perhaps her mother resented her daughter's departure from her side.

Another *"exiting"* by someone Doris loved.:(

Something had been going on with her mother that seemed to **PERSIST** to the present.

Doris appeared to be going through some psychological `adjustments` and Jana was concerned.

On the eve of her decision to go to Oklahoma, Jana called her mother to let her know she was going to see her and spend time with her.

To Jana's surprise her mother answered the phone...allowing Jana to bypass the usual message machine.

Doris sounded *unnaturally* happy to hear Jana's voice.

J a n a   t o o k   n o t i c e

Jana did not tell her mother the principal purpose of her visit; but let her know she wanted to spend some time with her and stay in the area for a while.

"I can see you at the airport and we'll drive home.", Doris happily said.

Jana responded, "No mom. I want to drive *alone* and take in the *air*".

Jana did not want her mother to bother in picking her up; and she really *did* want to take the time to do the sixty-one minute drive to Muscogee: a sort of re-initiation *spell*; a gestation back into the womb of where she came!; a formulation period to bring back tinges of emotions and discoveries (a backward journey spira*ling* into a forward journey: a *reshoot* of images with-a-mature-mind to manipulate the so called "destiny's" stubborn inclinations!...bringing the original plans to a close-of-intent; a breath-of-life resuscitating unfulfilled dreams replacing-them-fulfilled!)

příprava

Vorbereitung   筹备

h a z

i r

l

i k

с п и р а л л и н г

"Okay Honey!"

"But be careful and keep the air conditioner on since it is very **unusually** warm these days."

"I'll make use of the time to cook some nice entrée for you."

Jana was surprised that her mother would even mention cooking!

Growing up her mother rarely cooked since she was always off working odd hours as a nurse.

Usually, if she was lucky, Jana would receive take-out!

Most of the time, however, Jana was left on her own to cook her own food and many times Jana would cook for her mom as well...providing food for her when she arrived from work.

As the plane began its ^DE_SC_{ENT}, Jana felt a *SURGE OF POSSIBILITIES* inside her.

She was home!!!

!!

*H-*O M E**!**

*H-*O M E**!**

*H-*O M E！

A home she had sought to escape from....and now she was back!

B -A C K！

B -A C K！

B -A C K！

[dismantling in process]
[démantèlement
sökülmesi
purkaminen
демонтаж
tuuraki
demontaż
ভেঙে ফেলো
aftakeling]

Jana rented a 2007 Toyota *Camry* at the Avis stationed at the Airport.

She could have chosen something more flashy but Jana knew the reliability of a Toyota and their gas efficiency.

Jana also didn't want to increase Miguel's tab.

Besides, Jana did not seek to impress *no-one*.

As Jana pulled out of the Airport property, she noticed a **LARGE BIRD** *flying* above her.

At first she could not make out the type of bird; but once it descended in front of her she noticed it was a **HAWK**.

Jana found the bird's wings beautiful as it glided effortlessly in the mid-morning air.

And as Jana turned into the main highway to Muscogee, the hawk kept flying in front of her as if leading her **SOMEWHERE**.

SOMEWHERE leading leading **SOMEWHERE**

Jana found a strange connection to *that* bird. It was as though that bird knew her.

knew her knew her knew know her

Suddenly the hawk, having had communicated something to Jana, soared up higher ^and *higher* into the sky until she could no longer see it.

The open fields of Okla*homa* began to descend upon Jana during this early warm day.

The sky was clear: not a *cloud*-in sight!

As Jana took in the landscape, her *right* finger directed her hand towards the car's radio deck.

Jana flipped the radio *channels* looking for something looking for something looking for something.

All of sudden a *sound* captured her mind as it set into an **occupying space**.

Jana began to beat her *left* foot to the sound.

Jana heard the pumping bass drums accompanied by the rhythm of a ringing-electric-guitar coming from the car's *speakers*.

Jana turned up the sound and a voice began to enter her mind: it was the voice-of-Bono.

Jana paid attention to the words of Bono: "Don't believe what you hear. Don't believe what you see".

Jana felt a *spirituality* with that song as she understood more and more the significance of the arrangement of *those* words.

As Jana listened to the quartet: the *screeching*-guitar-solo came on and she felt like pushing-and-jumping-and-moving-violently all around as if to free herself from her *chains*.

Chains of Zoroastrianism **and the like**

Jana began doing hypnotic movements; her head started nodding back and forth as Bono began his sermon again.

Jana felt enlightened and Jana felt Hope and Faith; a Hope and Faith to find a *change*-in-her-life.

As the song faded, Jana turned-off-the-radio [turnedofftheradio] and began her mantra of *h*er-*o*wn-*m*usic while driving on the straight road ahead.

Jana began to breathe deeper while the vibrations of-her-music were felt inside her pupils: they seemed to vibrate with her heartbeat.

It was as though Jana delivered a natural dose of a benzodiazepine into her nervous-system; as if Jana unconsciously signaled the formation and deliverance of a drug into her human mind:

Jana began to *f*ade....

....slowly being transported somewhere beyond.....

Not aware that her past symptoms were taking over her...like a predator over its prey; like a *lion* species nation over a weaker developing species nation....

...such a devouring episode as that experienced in the Americas and in Asia and in the Entire World!

Jana began to *L-O S E* consciousness.

She began to be somewhere else and lost complete orientation of where-she-was.

Jana was in her heartbeat: streaming with the blood under the pressure of the heart: making s-l-o-w and r*a*-pid turns

r*a*-pid s-l-o-w turns turns r*a*-pid s-l-o-w.

Jana shrank within the **chaos-of-the-cells**...each vying for energy while attempting to work as a unit.

A rumbling sound began to shake her and Jana snapped out of her *trance* and found herself riding on a *d*irt *f*ield.

Jana screamed in startlement menstartled startledmen:

"Oh sh**it**!" "Oh sh**it**!" "Oh sh**it**!"

Slowly Jana recuperated the nerves-of-her-limbs and began to apply pressure on-her-foot.

The car began to slow and after a few seconds stopped.

There-*SAT*-Jana: breathing heavily.

"What was I thinking?!"

"Am I crazy?!"[yes]

"My baby is inside of me!"

"Be careful Jana!" she scolded herself.

"Be CAREFUL!!!!".

Jana closed her eyes and took one last deep breath before turning around to look for the *main-road*.

Jana could not tell where she was and could not find the road after a brief survey.

Jana got out of her car and felt the heat of this **unusual** fall midday pound-on-her.

Instead of resisting, Jana sought to be *one-with-the-heat* and to accept the heat as-her-friend (at least while she was chained to that body of hers...*a-body-belonging-to-the-*__HEAT__).

Suddenly Jana heard a **screech** from above.

Jana looked up and saw the *hawk* twirling around her.

Jana stared at it with blinking-eyes.

The __LARGE BIRD__ began to turn left and began to fly in *that* direction.

Instinctively Jana __KNEW__ to-follow-the-bird.

She got back into the car, turned it on, took another deep breath, and made a left toward the __HAWK__.

After about 3 minutes of following the hawk, Jana was able to view the <u>main-road</u>.

She drove toward it: then turned up onto it (making a right).

The **HAWK** was G O N E.

The rest of her road trip went without incident.

Jana cruised comfortably listening to the radio: looking at the clear sky and fields-of-open-space.

Jana let the environment *S*oak-*h*er-*s*enses.

She appreciated every-aspect-of-her-*drive*.

Jana **touched** her abdomen often on this trip: caressing her new creation inside of her [a new human creation with an old *eternal-mind-embedded*].

Jana talked to it often *telepathically*: telling it how much she loved it.

As the first *forty-five* minutes faded into memory, Jana turned off the air conditioner and opened the window to take in the natural heated air that surrounded her.

Jana now felt at-home in this environment: and the wind blowing into the car reminded her of the times when she took rides with mom and dad.

Times when all *three* had happy moments taking a trip to a lake or the Reservation or just to *go down* to get a *ba*nana sp*lit* Sunday.

*ba*nana sp*lit* Sunday

Those were playful times when dad was being silly: putting melted ice cream on everyone's face and laughing uncontrollably:

"My Sweets", he would say after he smothered "us" in cream and just fell into a ball-of-laughter!

Daughter and Mother proceeded likewise saying, "Sweet Dad!" and joined dad in his bout-of-laughter.

Jana LOVED-THOSE-DAYS.

.......how she mi*SS*ed-those-days.

....such memories that sustained her during the hard moments when Jana was stripped-from-their-presence.

As *9* minutes passed by: Jana saw the sign welcoming her to Muskogee.

Jana remembered the streets and pulled a right, about a mile from the sign, took a right to the 64 Business Hwy, and then a right to *Kala*mazoo Street then a left on 3rd St.: and there, at about *300* meters, on the right hand side, was her home.

The house had changed from when she moved out.

It had new dark *red* paint on it instead of the paling light *green* that was there before.

The windows were no longer the standard old small models with windowsills surrounding it.

The space was now occupied by an enlarged frame with a large modern weatherproof window:

which opened outward with a screen that appeared from the side as it opened.

The roof had changed from black-tar-tiles to Spanish red-roof-tiles.

Jana really did not notice the house at first: truly it was remodeled in a way that gave it a *new appearance*.

The next door neighbor's house, which had not changed, had a blue old paint, all weathered and chipping from the wooden frame, stood to the left of her house.

In fact, most of the houses had not changed but aged.

Jana pulled up to the drive way.

Immediately the front door opened.

There stood Doris Withirt Ó Coileáin, her mother, all smiles, and showcasing a beautiful flowered pink dress.

Jana also noticed that mother had changed her hair: bleaching and dying it *black*.

To Jana Doris looked very different: since her mother was a natural red head with orange freckles.

When Jana opened the car door, stood, and was about to walk toward the house, her mother shouted: "Wait Jana Wait!!!!"

Jana retracted a step and stood by the car door as her mother pulled out a portable digital camera and took several pictures of Jana by the rented *Camry*.

"I want this to be a beautiful memory for me darling, knowing you are home!"

After the snap shots by the *Camry*, Doris went to her daughter and embraced her lovingly.

Jana could not believe this beautiful unbecoming behavior from her mother. The last time Jana had received a hug from her mother was when Jana was 7 (while dad was still part of the family).

was was

Surprised Jana was happy and let loose her inhibitions and began to embrace her mother likewise.

Jana closed her eyes and took in her mother's embrace as-never-before.

For Jana, this was *genuine* physical love she had **not known** for a long time.

At that moment of **physical love**, it took Jana quite some time to accept it.

But once she did:

it-

was-

B E A U T I F U L

They held each other for a good 3 minutes and then Doris lead Jana to the house and showed her all the changes she had made to it.

When they reached Jana's room, nothing was changed: except for a new large window, light purple paint, and a modern Italian made queen size bed!!!! [oh-my-J!:)]

The room also smelled like Lavender.

Immediately Jana noticed that Lavender flowers were placed in three small glass containers: each looked like a heart shape that opened up at the top like a flower.

One was placed on her desk, another near the door, and yet another by her bed.

The afternoon went beautifully! :)

Doris cooked an extravagant shrimp-lasagna with spinach, garlic, and fresh tomatoes.

This was not purchased lasagna! [oh-my-J!-AGAIN!:)]

Doris had taken the time to make real home-made lasagna for this very special occasion she felt in her *heart*.

Doris served this with a *C*ool-*r*ed-*W*ine filled 3/4ths in *crystal* wine glasses.

On a flowery Colombian flat bowl, Jana saw another food she was not familiar with and asked...

"Mom! What are those ringy-things that look like shrimp!?"

"Those D*ear* are my version of *T*aralli bread with a hint of nutmeg and cinnamon."

"They come from the Italians and so I found a recipe for them and decided to make them this morning for us to enjoy!:)"

Yes Enjoy!:) Jana thought.

Doris continued:

"They are special little creatures conjured up by the Italians."

"After you prepare the dough the way that is pleasing to your imagination, you boil them and then bake them."

"Take one and *dip* it into your w*ine* my love"

Jana picked one-of-these **curious** little breads, dipped-it into her red wine, and then she *s l o w l y* took-it into-her-mouth while simultaneously breathing in the *invisible* fumes created by the wine.

Jana then paused and closed her eyes and took a *deep* breath.

Then she opened her eyes and said:

"Wow! It's great mom! Thanks!"

Doris smiled.

"I am learning to cook something different every week. It is sort of a period of discovery and creativity for me."

"I discover something new and then make it my own by modifying the recipe a bit....either cooking it slightly different or very different, or adding some additional ingredient idea that p*ops* into my head."

Jana smiled.

"I am so happy for you mom! I'm glad you're taking the time *to* discover n*e*w thi*n*gs to *d*o in your *life*!:)"

At about 3:31 p.m., they both decided to take a walk outside along the prairie nearby that had beautiful oak, osage-orange and sugarberry trees.

At first there was quietness and no one said a word.

It seemed that both wanted to **take-in-the-moment** in a way that allowed for deep breathing and thankfulness.

Both women had their difficult moments in life and both were grateful for being alive to continue to **sort out** their affairs.

Doris had turned cold emotionally to cope psychologically after Wild Feather left them. Doris really found it difficult to cope with such a **REMOVAL-CHANGE** ...from the person she loved deeply.

And when Jana moved out to go to college, Doris was again STRUCK with yet another difficult **REMOVAL-CHANGE**.

λ λ λ   λ   λ λ λ

[SUCH SUCH SUCH a **Removal Change** scenario is continually played out in this **strange world**!]

[A blatant **mockery** to eternity!]

[A continuously non-stop **deceitful** and **hurtful** ritual at a **BLINDED POPULACE** set by the **bodiless Enemy** in order to create confusion to break continuity!]

[We got to BE CAREFUL with the **enemy**'s and its physical **minions**' tricks that constantly seek and destroy relationships…creating a spiral affect hitting many souls in one shot!]

[The solution is discipline, perseverance, and a sound understanding of Jesus Christ! (love). We need to **RESIST!**]

λ λ λ   λ   λ λ λ

Being with Wild Feather made Doris feel safe.

Doris was madly in love with Jana's father and never wanted it to end.

Never To End!

And it did end to her surprise, making it **too overwhelming** for her to even talk in normal conversations at work or at home.

The **damage** of separation caused a shock to Doris' nerves...the change was the breaking point for Doris, who had previously endured the permanent, harsh separation from her parents...by death!!!

Doris felt she could no longer hold to anything...

ANYTHING!

NOTHING NADA HİÇBİR ŞEY DEĞİL

Doris felt that **the floor was moving non-stop!**…she was slipping more and more out into a void that frightened her. She became psychologically scared to the point of death!

How could Doris reconcile?

She could not! No! She could not!!!

Doris had based all her Hope and Faith onto this man she loved…loved enough to bear the fruit called Jana…and now this fruit had parted as well.

The synapses and all the connective tissue surrounding her mind were heading in opposite directions! *!* ❗ */!*

…Doris was losing her Sanity by the complete and constant removal of her family!!!

During those times Doris was losing the ability to function even at a moderate acquaintal level.

Doris just wanted to sleep and forget about everything.

Doris knew Jana needed more affection as a child, but back then she could not provide that:

ssomething grabbed hold of her!!!...as if protecting her from her emotions that were leading to suicide!!!

Doris became emotionally cold in order to cope and not die! Confused she became.

Doris could not sort out her confusing thoughts that grew in **multiples of intensity**:

especially at **night**.

SHE WAS OVERWHELMED!!!

That is why Doris had opted to take the night shifts at work and sleep during the day while her daughter was at school.

There was little contact but that was all Doris could give at that moment in those painful pasts.

Doris had no one to guide her.

[the best guidance is the Jesus Christ! Doris did not know Jesus Christ her savior then.]

Back then Doris became a 'living' lost soul!!!

But NOW was different!

NOW here was Mother and Daughter, reunited again after such a long break.

....each wanting to mend since each now had

the mental strength

and the mental nourishment received by intimate contacts with a Significant Other who truly cared!

Other Significant Significant Other.

Now was the time for reconciliation!

Now was possible!

Now was Hope!

Now was Faith!

Now was here!!!!

HERE EXISTING NOW!

NOW WAS HERE!!!!

After a very comfortable 12 minutes of silence between the walking pair, Doris spoke:

"Darling, I want to share some good news and I also want to express myself to you like I haven't done before."

Jana kept quiet and kept looking at the path: wanting to give her mother as much space as she needed to speak.

"First, I want to apologize for being very distant from you. I know you needed me *more* but I could not put myself to being *more* responsible and giving *more* of myself to you growing up."

"I am confessing this now to you Jana because I love you and because I want to move on from hang-ups of my past."

"I want to have a new life and I know *My-Beautiful* that you have always been so patient with me: even when you were too young to be it!"

"My confession is that I've always loved your father more than I could ever express to you; he was my life; my savior at a difficult time in my life when I had very little love and affection in my life."

"As you know, grandpa and grandma were taken away from me so early in life that I missed them so so so much!" "And I still do!"

"And, when your father came; he filled that void and more!"

"That is why darling when your daddy left I-COULD-NOT-COPE!!!"

"I-COULD-NOT-COPE!!!", tears streamed from Doris' eyes.

"When that separation happened I felt as though a dagger had struck my stomach and left there...slowly being continuously turned and destroying my insides: I was in constant pain of missing him!...Missing having him by my side."

"Missing him and not being able to take the dagger from my own flesh."

"I felt he could *only* remove it!"

"...Remove it as he once did for me when we first met."

[so in essence he placed-the-dagger-back!?]

"Many times, I contemplated ending my life and came close to it several times."

"I wanted that INTENSITY-OF-LOST-to-*end*!"

Jana had not known that her mother wanted to end her life.

Jana knew her mother was unhappy but never imagined she would even think of doing such a drastic decision.

Jana kept quiet.

Her mother continued:

"But the past is the past and I have Faith and I have Hope that you can forgive me for not being there for you darling."

Jana spoke up immediately:

"Mom, you don't *need* to apologize. I knew daddy leaving us caused you much pain as it had caused me."

"I love you mommy and I will always love you."

As Jana said these last two words, streams of tears rushed through her eyes and to the *ground*.

Doris grabbed her hand to stop her from walking and embraced her daughter.

Both cried streams of tears as sisters would in **times-of-realizations.**

At the conclusion of their embrace, the wordless-Silence was broken:

"I've met someone!" Doris spurted out.

"That is wonderful mommy; who is *he*?"

Doris responded:

"It"

"is"

"a"

"she".

A stressful *P a u s e* ensued in the being-of-Jana.

Streams of Coldness rushed through her being.

Doris sensed it.

Hec!!! Doris anticipated it even before she opened her mouth.

But Doris needed to *come-clean* about something as important as presenting her present-significant-other (who meant so much to her) to her own *flesh-and blood*: her daughter.

Jana was completely caught off guard by this information:

"A....she!?!" :-c :c :-
<a!!!!!!!!!!!!!!!!!!!!!!!!!!!!!

oooO00........   C;(<<<<woooo!<<<<
                        D:< Dingbat
                        <:-| awawawawawa!

                        ඊ_ඊ uuuufff!!!!
        (• • ;)   ((+_+))   (+o+)

        (°- °)   (• •?   <'∧'>

                ....   (l'o'l) >>>>>? WaiT_{ttt}

    (´＿ `) ....?!?!?!?!?!?!?!?!?!?!?!?!?!?!?
ouuouuouuuuuu
        ....   (*￣m￣) ....aaaeiii eheee aaaeiii!

This unorthodox openness caused a sudden bout-
of-*tings* in Jana (she immediately recalled the
day she was raped by that huge woman in the
college locker room).

""SUN-of-A>- ..>.>"""

She felt a bit disturbed at her mother's disclosure.

[a bit!!! that's an underSTATEMENT!!!
come-o0n now Mi'Kha-el!!]

['okay']

Never *ever* would she imagine such a thing coming from her mother.

Jana tried to hide her reaction but it was plain to...

See!!!

See!!!

See!!!

"Listen darling I know this must be freaking you out right now [well...yea!]: but it is true."

"I've found this beautiful woman who loves me and I love her!"

"We've known each other for about seven months; she is my coworker at the hospital."

Jana tried hard to resolve her issues as to a *S*ame-*S*ex-*P*artner coming into her mother's life.

It was hard enough for Jana thinking as a child that her daddy may one day be replaced by another **man!**

But that fear-of-replacement had subsided in Jana for a good while now.

Jana had made up her mind in her mid-twenties that her mother needed someone and that it was not right for her to be ALONE-AND-UNHAPPY.

But, having a woman as a partner took-some-getting-use-to for Jana.

F atuus I nflamator!

Jana could not find the words to try to give her approval to her mother. [What Approval!@@!??]

As much as Jana tried she just kept silent and took **deep** breaths.

Jana was *freaked-Out!*

Doris interrupted Jana's **deep** breaths:

"Let's change the subject darling. What is new with you?"

"What new adventures have you experienced?"

There was a silence from both *again* and this time both just kept silent for a GooD while.

The ***only-sound*** being heard were the *chirps* of the birds *surrounding* them.

It seemed as though the birds had agreed to provide some-soundtrack to *drown-out-* the-silence.

Both women had been through tough times and both wanted to be careful with each other: both wanted the relationship to grow. Both cared *deeply* for one another.

"Mommy, I want to be honest with you. I am caught by surprise and please forgive me for not being outright happy for you **in-an-instant**."

"It's just that it is taking me *some-time* to take in your announcement."

"It is taking me *a working* to block out prejudices which **H***inder* my happiness for your announcement."

Jana was QUICK in her words.

In her mind, each word was *carefully chosen* as she spoke.

"Regardless of my first reaction mom,"

Stiffness entered her abdominal muscles.

A pause.

She breathed **HEAVY** again and somehow relaxed the tension within her.

"I accept and welcome that you have welcomed another *human being* to love you."

[*feee*uuu...dat was challenging! Yup!]

" I do love you mommy and I am happy for you. Please give me some time to take-it-in! *in.*"

"As you wait to hear from me to discuss in depth your new relationship: keep in mind that regardless of my prejudices mommy: I am happy for you because I want YOU MOMMY to be happy."

Jana's mother nodded with understanding.

Doris knew that even the so-called **modern world** had difficulty understanding intimate *true-love* regardless-of-sex.

Many understand and many **do-not understand** that *Love* exists in-abundance **everywhere** because any-type-of-true love is *truly* SEXLESS!

SEXLESS

Both continued their *strides* through the prairie feeling satisfied with their own reactions.

Even though an amicable *eye-to-eye* on the subject was presently opposite and placed and allowed to be placed in *dormant*, a breath of fresh air **brushed** their faces.

Jana walked fiddling with A THOUGHT: she *expanded* it and *contracted* it in her mind.

...It was as though she were playing with a *yo-yo*: the same THOUGHT through one-loop and then through another and then a return for a new cycle.

Jana began to speak of this THOUGHT:

"Mommy, I have far too many things that have happened to me; but I want to share some of my important *new-new*s!".

Jana took a deep breath and swayed her arms further apart as if attempting to stretch.

After the *seventh-stride*-from-**that**-point-of-reference she spoke:

"I am *pregnant* mommy and the man of my dreams is the father. I don't know the sex of the baby; but I do know that the baby is safe and healthy."

Jana clumped all those additional ideas into one single idea....bringing forth a sort of awkward CRUNCH-OF-WORDS:

new news
Pregnant
man of my dreams
sex and health of baby

.......as if not knowing how to take the time to present one idea and expand it, *before* proceeding to the next.

Maybe Jana **supposed-it-to-be** a *summary?*; or an *abstract* of her ideas?; or a *synopsis* of something she wanted to elaborate?; or a *résumé* yet to be completed?; or a *précis* of a well-rehearsed idea?

Whatever the *intent*, Jana continued to speak:

"I came to Oklahoma to see you mommy because I love you. But I also came to learn more of my father's family and my ancestral roots."

Jana hesitated: creating a silent pause.

After *seven* seconds and *several* breaths, Jana continued:

"I want to know my roots and …"

Doris interrupted her (seeing Jana uneasy and hearing the repetition of the word "roots"):

"Darling, you have the right to know your roots and I respect that; it is just too bad I don't know my *OWN* roots....for that you would have to go to Ireland. But as to your father's roots: THEY ARE *here*."

"And as to you making me a grandma: *thank you Jana!*"

Doris looked at her daughter and her daughter looked at her mother and the grandmother looked at the grandchild within the abdomen:

All *three* **smiled** in *concert*!

The rest of the walk was pleasant.

Jana was satisfied that she had shared some of her motives for coming to Oklahoma (except of course those regarding her dreams, and the issues she has as to insomnia and bouts of sudden loss of consciousness).

The Jana trilogy novel continues on Book 3
subtitled:

Book 3 *of 3*
Dream Roads True Roads
The Legacy Unfolds!

. . . .

<u>Message from Mi'Kha-el Feeza:</u>

Mi'Kha-el Feeza WEBSITE:

Eternoi.Com

Buenos Días Reader!

Regeneration of Love and Resistance for the common good is working at my website. We are looking for like-minded individuals and organizations to collectively help rid ourselves of the ills of our communities in this world peacefully.

We seek to bring the betterment of the common good to the forefront of the consciousness of every single human being, A.I., and extraterrestrial. And in so doing, bring fruitful, constructive change, peacefully, to all of the world's and Earth's inhabitants for the benefit of all as a whole!

If you'd like to join one of our committees for the Regeneration of Love and Resistance…come visit and join!:) The more free minds the better! Together we are a Collective Mind that is bringing change to the world and the Earth for the betterment of the common good! We are Eternoi Humanitarian Organization (Eternoi).

We, Eternoi, believe there is a good fruitful solution to every ill in this world and on this planet! God gave us a mind to think! Let's use it for the common good! We are wholly

Volunteer Based. We never collect any monies directly into the organization as a whole. Any expenses to promote an Eternoi solution to a world ill are paid by each member, as to each member's own will and ability, directly to the service provider, vendor, etc. Example of expenses includes assembly permit fees, etc. Consequently and by design, every member of Eternoi is a volunteer, including the leadership. We, Eternoi, never solicit expense monies from anyone OUT OF the Eternoi membership body. Specific committees are involved in seeing which members are willing and able to help pay the Eternoi solution expenses, as described, directly to the service provider, etc.

And, Eternoi membership is always FREE. One becomes an Eternoi member after being successfully vetted to a specific committee. We believe in the goodness of every single human being. We believe that change for the betterment of the common good comes by example, encouragement, and by awareness!

Have Faith and have Hope and move forward in love!

May God the Father, who is in Heaven and within us, bless you always!

Sincerely,

Mi'Kha-el Feeza
eternoi@protonmail.com

ACKNOWLEDGEMENTS AND NOTES

All final output Images in the novel by the author. All Artwork in the novel by the author. All final versions images found in the novel created by the author. Origins of some raw images used as a base for artwork by the author originating from elsewhere in their raw original format noted below.

Only Raw Free Use Images (from pexels.com, pixaybay.com, et al.) or Raw Pubic Domain images used from their original format into the author's artwork where used in the novel, where final artwork arrangements of images where made by the author. All other images in the novel produced exclusively by the author.

The author would like to thank and acknowledge the following people for their contributions in preparing the novel for publication:

Craig Longshore from the Oklahoma Forestry Services at Sallisaw in 2015, Friday, October 5th. Thank you Mr. Longshore for your willingly professional and very friendly and helpful assistance in providing the author with vital data as to the most common native tree species found in the Muskogee County area.

The author would like to thank ALL THE MODELS found in the final artistic art format photographs produced by the author in this novel for presenting their God given bodily images willingly. ¡Gracias! ...y que Dios santísimo siga bendiciéndolos en donde se encuentren... ¡en ésta o la próxima vida!

Finally, thank you to these photographers for their free use original images used in the artwork by the author in this novel: Gerhard G; Sipa; Marcel Langthim; Thomas G; Cottonbro; Warren K Leffler; Polina Tankilevitch, Andrew; Ottoni Lu Ottoni; Andrea Piacquadio; Alvin C. Kraenzlein; H.Hach; Dan Evans; Andi Ravsanjani Gusma; Anete Lusi; Elijah O'Donnell; Luiz Fernando; Julia Volk; Rodnae Productions; Sam Lion; Hamed Almari; Quintin Gellar; Hassan Ouajbir; Ba Tik; Eunhyuk Ahn; David Mark; Armin Rimoldi; Artem Beliaikin; Victoria Boirodinova; Zorro Zombie; Heyn & Matzen image of Joseph Two Bulls; Erika Wittlieb; Ian Beckley; Miriam Espacio; Min An; João Cabral; Edward S. Curtis Piegan; John Vachon; Timothy H. O'Sullivan; Zinpix; Yan Krukov; Neto Soares; David De Giovanni;Alexander Krivitskiy; Bhargava Marripati; Raul Juarez; Ricardo Esquivel; Andreza Vasconcelos; Burak Fatih;Jonathan Borba; Katerina Holmes; Kathryn Archibald; Daria Shevtsova; Ketut Subiyanto; Matheus Bertelli; Meru Bi; Pavel Danilyuk; Anna Shvets; Tatiana Twinslol; Mateus Souza; and a thank you to the Brazilian National Archives; and Fenno Jacobs. ¡Gracias!

And thank you readers for taking the time to read something different!...and hopefully something that will help transform your lives to serve your community better, and to find contentment in small actions for a better world!

Sincerely,

Mi'Kha-el Feeza

This novel is also dedicated to
Karl Marx
A man who spoke the truth, and so eloquently wrote it despite hazards that presented themselves.

About The Author

No. The Author is not Full of Shit! [Well: maybe sometimes, temporarily, after eating:)]

The author is from Santa Monica, California. He is (among many things like most of us) a musician, visual artist, and literary writer. This may be his very first and very last writings in terms of "a novel" for many reasons that go beyond his control.

Mi'Kha-el Feeza is a graduate from the University of California, Los Angeles with a degree in history. He is also a graduate from Loyola Marymount University, Los Angeles with a master degree in education. Mi'Kha-el Feeza attended under an assumed name!

The author wishes to evidently EXPRESS his *will* to help every-single-human-being to be awaken from the deceptions of this world and conformity thereof (controlled by those in power who control all sources of communication) so that he and she may find *their true nature* AWAY FROM the prison bodies and world "we" are contained in: A world inhabited by entities forced into Carbon encasements for the *ultimate* purpose of extraction of one's energy.

oT eht stsinataS taht elur eht dlrow: potS gniyalp sa fi sretsefinam-fo-a-enod-laed. oN slaed evah neeb deifidilos; on sraw evah neeb now. oN egaugnal detaerc lliw reted na-dne-ot-ruoy-emag. cigaM dna sllepS era sloot fo a naicigam...a tcudorp fo eslaf sesimorp...a gniralf thgil gnimoc ot sti elzzif!

elzzif elzzif elzzif

tahW si fo nam? *tahW si fo* nuS? *tahW si fo* lasrevinU yrotirreT?: a mroftalp tuohtiw elbats dnuorg!

...A gnihsem fo seigrene ot eb ylenif desuffid dna denethgiarts ro⁼ gnissecorp kcab ot rieht *nigiro*....gnisol lla lortnoc fo noilleber.

noilleber: ylleb pu!

ehT seirotcaf era gnimoc ot a esolc...lla stnemele gnieb nekater roⁱ *eht-gnisolc-fo-eht-rood!*

ecnO eht rooD si tuhS...

...ereht si oN-nruteR

osergeron

Jesus Christ is the Only Way to True Salvation!

J

Jana was written by the author from 2007 to 2018, with final editorial revisions from 2019 to November 2020 (13 years of writing to complete) in the following locations:

- Harvey Bay, Queensland, Australia
- Santa Monica, California
- Malibu, California
- San Diego, California
- San Francisco, California
- Oahu, Hawaii
- Kauai, Hawaii
- Pacific Ocean, 700 miles from Kona on a Hawaiian Airlines Aircraft
- Tulsa, Oklahoma
- Tucson, Arizona
- Grand Junction, Colorado
- Baltimore, Maryland
- "Agantao" The Tin Can [my exile]
- Strange Town
- Crenshaw/Coliseum Streets in LA
- The Lazy Living Room: Larchmont Village

...villagers [these and the like around the world] you are allowed to Awaken! Look around you, breathe, and see beyond your own comforts! Yes villagers: others exist that need your help! ¡Vámonos! True Help Not Crumbs. Need an Incentive: By Helping Others You Help Yourselves! J

- City of Bell (one hour afternoon)
- Seattle, Washington
- Whittier, California